C000244524

I'm
New
Here

25/8
£1.50

I'm
New
Here

Ian
Russell-
Hsieh

SCRIBNER

LONDON NEW YORK SYDNEY TORONTO NEW DELHI

First published in Great Britain by Scribner,
an imprint of Simon & Schuster UK Ltd, 2024

Copyright © Ian Russell-Hsieh, 2024

SCRIBNER and design are registered trademarks of The Gale Group, Inc.,
used under licence by Simon & Schuster Inc.

The right of Ian Russell-Hsieh to be identified as author of
this work has been asserted in accordance with the
Copyright, Designs and Patents Act, 1988.

1 3 5 7 9 10 8 6 4 2

Simon & Schuster UK Ltd
1st Floor
222 Gray's Inn Road
London WC1X 8HB

Simon & Schuster: Celebrating 100 Years of Publishing in 2024

Simon & Schuster Australia, Sydney
Simon & Schuster India, New Delhi

www.simonandschuster.co.uk
www.simonandschuster.com.au
www.simonandschuster.co.in

A CIP catalogue record for this book
is available from the British Library

Trade Paperback ISBN: 978-1-3985-2288-6
Ebook ISBN: 978-1-3985-2289-3
Audio ISBN: 978-1-3985-3044-7

This book is a work of fiction. Names, characters, places
and incidents are either a product of the author's imagination or
are used fictitiously. Any resemblance to actual people living or
dead, events or locales is entirely coincidental.

Typeset in Palatino by M Rules
Printed and Bound in the UK using 100% Renewable
Electricity at CPI Group (UK) Ltd

FOR ELLIE

ONE

Maybe it was the durian.

The durian that smelt like a septic tank when the little guy with the stained wifebeater and one tooth hacked it open with a cleaver.

Some people think it's the best smell in the world, you know that?

Me? My guts were revolting before I even put the thing in my mouth.

It slips up and out, easy as anything. With every strobe that slices the dark, I see it lit up on the front of my shirt.

For true, looks like a Jackson Pollock.

No one has noticed, though.

Nope. They're just pulsing in the rainbow lights.

Human stop-motion.

Dancing in their awkward Asian way.

Thump, thump, thump, thump.

A four-four bass drum punches my speedbag heart.

Maybe it was the booze. No, one hundred percent it was the booze. A bucket's worth of Kaoliang, beer and whisky sloshing around my insides along with the fruit and my dinner.

Here comes another wave.

Oh look, I've made the floor all slippy, and now I'm on my arse.

A jungle of bare legs in stilettos stomps, rises, falls. Legs in trousers too, but who gives a shit about those, eh? A flash of lacy underwear under a tight skirt and . . .

Nothing.

I feel nothing. Which, come to think of it, isn't so bad.

Have a drink, Sean, let go, lose control for once. That's what you always say.

I bet you never thought you'd be able to get me hammered like this – like those idiots at the A&E in Euston that one Saturday night.

Remember?

Your face swelled up like a balloon that night, and man did we laugh about it.

Congrats, Mia. I'm doing what you wanted.

I'm living my life, on the floor, covered in my own bile.

I hope you're fucking happy.

* * *

I wake up, alone.

The TV is on at low volume. My tongue is a fat, dried slug and a million tiny devils are busting into my skull with teeny-weeny hammers and teeny-weeny chisels.

I open my eyes and push myself upright.

Dull light through closed curtains.

I look down. Naked from the waist up.

Why are my trousers damp? I smell old sweat and the vinegar reek of sick.

My phone says 9:48 am.

I close my eyes and I lie back down and I remember where I am.

Shit, breakfast.

I grab my T-shirt from the floor and run out the room.

* * *

Weird tasting tea.

Congealed eggs, rubbery sausages, shrivelled tomatoes and soggy toast.

Classic, budget hotel breakfast. The kind of hotel businessmen check into for somewhere cheap and clean.

I don't remember getting back here last night. I do remember going to a club. What was the name?

Continuum.

A wanky name for a swanky place you would never catch me at in London.

No playing, there's nothing that says 'sad bastard' more than going to a club on your own.

I need to go back to bed.

* * *

Someone is at my table. One of the hotel staff, arms folded. She's dressed in a navy-blue skirt and a wrinkle-free white blouse, hair tied up in a bun. I look at her blankly.

What are you doing here? she says in English. American-tinted English, like most Taiwanese. Her face crumples. And what is that smell?

I look down at my trousers, then my food. Breakfast, I say.

She says, And how is it?

Not great, I say. You should tell management.

Her eyes become slits. You really don't remember me, do you?

I push my eggs around. Refresh my memory?

A few weeks ago. We met at that bar with the floating lanterns, did karaoke, I invited you back to my place. We had sex.

We did? Was I good?

No.

Then what happened?

You stole from me, she says.

Okay. That took a weird turn. The way I see it, I now have two options.

One: tell this girl she's got the wrong guy, gag my breakfast down and go sightseeing.

Or two: pretend I am this thief she thinks I am, tell her of course I remember her. Ethically questionable, but what the hell.

Of course I remember you, I say. I put on my charming smile and nudge her on the arm. What did I take again?

Do you remember my name? You were shouting it enough, she says, dusting off the spot on her arm where I touched her.

I say, I'm pretty bad at names.

She says, Enjoy your meal, sir.

I get to thinking about those Antarctic emperor penguins who live in minus-fifty-degree conditions, and how they would for sure enjoy the chill coming off this girl.

She pivots and walks back to her post at the front desk, each sharp click of her heels stabbing my poor, soft, squidgy brain.

Two

I wake up, alone.

My phone says 2:16 pm.

I look around the room properly for the first time. Small TV sat on a built-in desk. Mini-fridge under that. To my left, a tiny hallway and a shower room. To my right, a window with an armchair to the side.

Everything is white.

Maybe more grey, actually. On the walls, generic, over-saturated photographs of Taipei landmarks.

There's the 101 building in the middle of a sunset.

Over there is an elaborate temple – gold, red and blue.

And over there—

No. This is the most heinous thing I've ever seen in my life.

A photo with actual light trails made from car taillights.

Who takes these pictures?

For real, there are horrific things I can kind of

understand. Skintight trousers on fat men. Non-alcoholic beer. Old folks who drive fancy sports cars at forty miles an hour on the motorway.

But light trail photographs?

To make up for the massive *Fuck You Sean* on the wall, I grab my camera out of my bag, walk over to the window and draw the curtains.

Heavy, grey skies. Tall, grey buildings. Not a landscape to take your breath away, just the kind I like. Down there, Taipei simmers under its tight lid of clouds.

Camera to my face, I frame and shoot, then push the film advance with my thumb. The whir and the click of the lever soothes me.

Shooting film, it's reassuring. You've got to know how to expose your picture properly. You have to understand the relationship between the shutter speed and the aperture and the rating of the film. You have to take into account the lighting conditions.

You only have thirty-six shots (even less if you're shooting medium format), so you have to make every single frame count.

And if you're a real photographer, you have to learn how to process and print your film with your own hands.

Take away the digital crutches of your average photographer's phone or camera, and they wouldn't know what the hell to do.

And that, well, that makes me feel good.

There's this photograph by Elliott Erwitt, *Bratsk Wedding*. In it, there's a young couple waiting to get married, sitting on a row of chairs in a registry office. Next to them, a smooth, handsome young white dude in a suit.

This dude, he's smiling, looking at something out of frame.

And this couple, they're staring at this dude like he just slept with the bride.

Shot with his trusty Leica M3 on Tri-X 400, a frigging documentary masterpiece.

Why is the guy smiling like that? What the hell is happening?

Stories for days.

I sit down in the armchair and rest my camera on my lap. Now what?

Back to bed, that's what.

Someone knocks on the door – three short, sharp raps. I get up and look through the spy hole.

The girl from breakfast.

She pushes past me as I open the door, no hello, no nothing.

Nice underwear, she says, perching herself on the edge of the bed. I don't know many guys who wear lilac briefs.

* * *

My monkey is limp. The condom comes off, goes into a tissue and gets chucked at the bin. I miss.

The front desk girl gets up and turns the shower on. Steam drifts and swirls through the open door.

I would never normally go for an Asian girl, they're not my type. But sex with this girl was a whirlwind. More one-sided than not, which suited me just fine.

I try and wave the image of Mia's face beneath mine away, but it won't budge. Sex with Mia was for sure less of a whirlwind. More intense though.

Fact: she's the only person I've ever come with at the same time.

Anyway, who gives a shit? Shooting my load is shooting my load. Better with a girl on top of me than into my hand, that's what I say.

The girl is out the shower. A white towel wrapped around her body, another one piled up high on her head. She walks to the armchair by the window and sits, staring at me.

You were better the first time, she says.

(Of course he was.)

I say, Well that makes two of us then.

Remember my name yet?

Sorry.

She sighs. It's Akemi.

I say, Akemi, right.

Deciding she's had enough chit-chat, she bends down to pick up her neat pile of folded clothes. I enjoy watching her get dressed. Deliberate in the way she moves, easing her panties on, then her bra, then her skirt, her blouse, and finally her heels.

She checks herself in the mirror, twirling her hair around back into the bun she wore this morning.

Eyes still locked on her reflection, she says, See you later, then.

You don't want the thing I stole from you back? I ask.

The door clicks shut behind her.

THREE

My phone says 9:10 pm, four and a bit hours after Akemi left my room.

Outside, the city is starting to light up – streetlights, car lights, neon lights.

Aeroplanes drag their blinking red dots across the night sky. Over there, a satellite draws a golden, sweeping line on its way around the earth.

I tried to go back to sleep after Akemi left. It didn't work. So I just lay on the bed and watched TV.

Old repeats of *Quantum Leap* dubbed in Mandarin. Taiwanese soap operas in Hokkien with swooning females and dramatic music. Period wuxia films with half-bald, half-ponytailed guys flying through bamboo forests. A late-night news bulletin featuring an old hoarder man surrounded by piles and piles of handwritten letters. Another late-night news bulletin featuring rows and rows of Chinese tanks, then footage of a missile launch, all apocalyptic fire and smoke. Adverts for McDonald's that look exactly like the adverts for McDonald's back home.

I speak fluent non-Hokkien, and even more fluent non-Mandarin, so all I'm left with is a bunch of flashing pictures and a made-up commentary in my head.

I get off the bed and take a piss. I sniff. I smell like the inside of Akemi.

Time for a shower, I guess. It's been a few days.

* * *

Thanks for using up all the hot water, Akemi, I love cold showers.

I towel myself dry and look around my new make-shift home – the puke-covered trousers from last night, collapsed in the corner. The used condom tissue, lurking around the wastepaper basket. Crumpled crisp packets of exotic flavours, sprinkled around the floor in between the crushed beer cans.

Wait, there's still a crisp in this packet.

I munch. Lobster and seaweed flavour, nice.

This hotel room is starting to depress me. I could, theoretically, be doing all this luxurious living in a Premier Inn down the road from our flat in London.

* * *

Taipei boils me as I walk.

The smell of rotten eggs. A stench stifled by a nose pinch when I used to visit as a kid with my parents.

It radiates from the pavement, from the buildings, from the toxic exhaust pipes sput-sput-sputtering on the road.

A thick haze covers the city at night, making everything look soft and blurry round the edges.

Mia uses this word I'd never heard before: 'close'. I laughed the first time she said it: What the hell does that mean?

She told me to bugger off.

Now I get it. The word was created for this place in the middle of summer. A billion little spheres of sweat bubble and trickle down my brow, my nose, my neck, my back, my crack. My feet stick to my socks, my socks stick to my shoes.

Traveller rule number one: explore the neighbourhood you're staying in. This one here, right now, nothing special.

Beat-up electronics shops, worn-out restaurants, signs of us western raiders: Starbucks, Ben & Jerry's, H&M.

My stomach whines.

Across the street, a giant pink doughnut with arms and eyes sits on top of a cafe, its puny legs dangling over the side. *Monsieur Donut, the best donuts in town!* glows the sign.

There's only so much crisps and beer can do for you.

A coffee and a doughnut should provide better nutrition. I wait for a gap in the traffic, cross the road and walk in.

* * *

The chill hugs me and my body goes limp like I've been constipated for weeks and I just, finally, had the biggest dump ever.

Everything is bright. Stark white walls and pink booths. A plinky-plonk muzak version of 'Looking with My Eyes' plays quiet on the speakers.

There's a free table by the window, so I go to the counter and the zit-blasted boy behind it, point to a picture on the laminated menu, take an age to count out the unfamiliar money, and sit down before anyone else can walk in and grab my seat.

While I wait, I think about Akemi. How is it that she thinks I'm someone she slept with a few weeks back?

Across the street, I see a guy in the darkness, moving away, calling after someone: *Guo lai!*

Seductive and singing and sly.

Shadows pass under an infinity of blinking neon signs, ill-looking taxi drivers cruise around for their next fare, and nighttime in Taipei unravels slow.

Scooters. So many scooters.

FOUR

Do you mind if I sit here?

The man standing there with a tray in his hands is in his sixties. Handsome – for an East Asian, anyway – in your classic fifties movie star kind of way. He's wearing a suit Cary Grant would look good in.

His hair though, I've never seen hair so white. Not a little bit grey, not a little bit silver. White. Like white–cotton wool white.

Yes mate, I say. I mind very much.

He says, I promise I won't bother you. Your table is the only table with a free seat. Three, to be exact.

I look around, and he's not wrong.

I say, Okay, and I drag my bag off the table slow, as slowly as I can.

He watches patiently. When the bag is finally on the

seat next to mine, he sits down in the chair diagonally opposite me.

Much obliged, he says.

I bite a chunk out of my doughnut and stare out the window. 10 pm and this city shows no sign of slowing. Scooters buzz, people swarm, shop lights blaze.

Everything is alien. The signs in Chinese characters, the traffic, the people.

Everyone looks like me: black hair, slanted eyes. For once in my life, I don't stick out.

For true though, these people aren't the same as me. They walk different, carry themselves different, talk and act and gesture different. They live different.

Here I am, surrounded by 'my people', yet I've never felt more out of place in my life. I knew it back when I was a kid, and no playing, I know it now.

It's around lunchtime in England. Mia's probably sitting in the park in front of the gallery. Maybe in the shade of a big tree, eating last night's leftover pasta. Maybe reading a book, if she isn't with her friends from the studio.

Say, is that a Leica? The man is looking at my camera.

I ignore him, carry on looking out the window.

An M2? he says.

I turn to face him. Look, mister—

I have an M3, he says.

Dabbled with photography a little while ago, he says.

Wasn't ever very good to tell you the truth, he says, but it's a beautiful machine. Engineered close to perfection – every little detail has a purpose. Nothing is wasted or superfluous.

You've got to admire that level of precision, he says. Oh, and the film advance lever, there's something so ... soothing about the act of pushing it, wouldn't you agree?

It's only now that I realize the man's English is perfect. Unlike everyone else here, he has an English accent, with a hint of the Midlands in there.

I give in. What's with your accent?

He smiles. Ah, I went to university in Birmingham – lived there for eight years. My girlfriend at the time was from Birmingham, too.

I'm thinking, this is crazy; Birmingham is an hour from where I grew up. As a kid, I used to go there with my parents all the time.

He says, I don't have to be a detective to guess that you're a photographer – especially with an old film camera like that.

I don't get on with digital cameras, he says. They strip the soul out of photography. With film, you're affecting the photographs with your hands. And the smell of the chemicals in the darkroom, there's nothing like it.

I bite another chunk out of the doughnut, and I can't help but think this guy gets it.

What kind of photography do you do? he says.

Street and documentary, I say.

I'm going to get another doughnut, he says. Do you want one?

I shrug, and off he goes to the counter.

When he comes back, he's carrying an entire platter of doughnuts – eight of them – all different types and flavours. And two more coffees. The one he places in front of me is black, just how I like it.

He sits down, this time in the chair directly opposite mine.

Please, he says, help yourself.

I take one that looks like it's been filled with jam. Sometimes, you can't go wrong with the classics.

This might seem a little forward, the man says, but would you consider doing a job for me? You see, I've always believed that things happen for a reason, call it fate or destiny, and so it's no coincidence that I bump into a photographer in a cafe – precisely at the time I'm in need of a photographer's services.

I pour sugar into my cup, looking to see if he's having me on, but all I see is a deep earnestness radiating.

I say, How do you know I don't already have a job?

And he says, I know the look of someone who's down

on their luck. Believe me, I've been there myself. Also, you're clearly not from here.

I don't take commissions from private clients, sorry.

Ah, artistic integrity, he says, I like that. What if I pay you handsomely for your services?

I say, How much is 'handsomely'?

Let me ask you a question, he says, putting his elbows on the table, clasping his hands together. How much would you charge a magazine for an assignment?

He's so far forward his nose is nearly touching mine and I have to lean back to make some space.

It doesn't work like that, I say. They have a set rate; I accept it or I don't.

How much?

I pick up my camera and handle the smooth, curved metal. Play with the focus ring while I figure out what number to tell the guy.

A thousand pounds for a series of pictures.

He leans back in his chair again.

I'll pay you two thousand pounds.

He takes a card from his inner jacket pocket and tosses it onto the table.

I pick up the card. *CHARLES HU*, reads the name, embossed in gold on a plain, off-white background. The texture of the card on my fingers feels expensive. Patrick Bateman would flip the fuck out.

Other than the name, there's nothing else on the card. No company, no job title, no number. I flip the card over to see if there's anything on the back, but it's blank.

Think about it, he says, knowing and confident and smiling.

FIVE

How that night was supposed to work, while Mia was at the gallery, I was gonna clean the place up real nice.

Cook her favourite meal (steak, mushrooms, chimichurri), blow up some balloons, hide behind the door and scare the shit out of her when she came in.

Because who doesn't like surprises?

Only when I jump out and shout, Happy birthday!, she's dripping wet from the rain and her eyes have bags under them and she looks tired and not right at all.

I say, Are you okay?

And she says those words that nobody in the history of the world wants to hear: Can we talk?

Now the balloons and the cake and the food on the table letting off swirls of steam look sad and, for true, like some sort of joke.

She takes off her drenched trench coat and sits down on the sofa.

She says, What's going on with you?

And I say, What do you mean what's going on with me?

And she says, You got fired from the paper, and now all you do is stay inside playing video games. You don't shower. You don't get dressed. You eat junk all day. You don't even make it nice in here for when I get home from work.

She says, You don't see your friends. You never want to do anything with me at the weekend. Do you know how frustrating that is?

Me, I'm crossing my arms, lining up all the things I can say to obliterate this argument and win.

And I say, What are you talking about? I point to the stupid balloons and the stupid cake and the stupid clean flat.

And I say, Also, we went for a curry across the road the other week.

And I say, Also, I saw Ed at his screening on Thursday. He says hi, by the way.

She stares at me. We don't have sex anymore. It's been nearly a year.

I know this is true, because for the last ten months (not a year, actually), I've spent my days beating my monkey to internet porn behind closed curtains, and when Mia gets home and she starts to get even a little bit intimate, I don't feel like it.

And I say, That's a lie and you know it.

She says, Have you thought about talking to someone?

I laugh, because that is clearly a ridiculous idea.

Mia sighs and she says, I'm being serious. You used to have energy for me. For fun. Now you're a gaping black hole, and you're sucking up all *my* energy.

She says, I feel mad at you all the time, and I don't want to feel like that.

She says, I don't know if I can do this anymore.

I'm thinking, Why is she attacking me like this?

And then I grab my jacket and my keys, and I say, Then don't.

And as I'm about to go out the door, I say, You know why we don't have sex? Because you got *fat*.

I'm not proud of it, but it is what it is.

SIX

A plinky-plonk muzak version of 'Looking with My Eyes' plays quiet on the speakers.

The next night, and I'm back at Monsieur Donut. The same music on loop all day, the same striplight glare, the same customers – no wonder Zit Boy behind the counter looks like he's about to off himself.

Death by doughnut.

The cafe is just as busy as it was yesterday. Everything is the same. Good.

Who has a business card with just a name and no contact details, anyway?

Wait. Everything is the same, except the table me and Charles Hu were sitting at by the window yesterday – there's a couple there, holding hands, staring into each other's eyes like a pair of retarded morons.

I go up to them and stand there. Just stand there, like I just recovered from some serious head trauma but I'm not all there anymore.

Staring at them with my mouth open and my tongue lolling out.

The young guy looks up at me. Picture a nerd – thick-lensed wire-frame glasses, long hair parted right down the centre and seasoned with little flecks of dandruff – not the kind to start something, that's for sure.

I don't even look away, I don't even move an inch.

What I do, I start making this low, rumbling sound that comes from my gut.

I drool a little, making sure the string of saliva oozes onto the table.

Overkill, maybe, but you can't half-arse these things.

The young guy, he has no idea what to do, he's never seen anything like it. He's just staring at me, thinking through his options.

Before he can do anything though, his girl stands up and grabs his arm. He glides back and away from the table.

Why is he sitting on a chair with wheels?

Oh.

Ah well. Table now free, I sit down and wait.

See? Act crazy, no one messes with you.

It's quarter to ten, fifteen minutes before Charles Hu

appeared out the blue yesterday and asked if he could sit with me.

There's a half-eaten doughnut and a Coke left on the table, so I munch, and I slurp, and I kill me some time.

* * *

Do you mind if I sit here?

My watch says 10 pm.

I wouldn't be here if I minded, I say.

He takes a seat in front of me. The white hair threw me yesterday, I guessed he was in his sixties. Looking at him now, I think I was a decade over.

It's the eyes – they're slick and bright and they shine. You know, like the way little kids' eyes shine.

Another sharp suit he's got on. Navy this time, hanging perfect on a body that's lean like a featherweight's.

He just sits there, looking at me. Smiling.

I sit there, looking at him.

Ah, here they come, he says.

And just then, Zit Boy brings a platter of eight dough-nuts to the table. Musty body odour wafts out of his short sleeves and gets stuck at the back of my throat.

Please, says Charles, Charlie, Mr Hu. An open hand, palm up, points towards the platter. A thin rectangu-lar watch with a black crocodile leather strap peeks out of his cuff. Nothing chunky, or extravagant. But expensive-looking.

A pink one with sprinkles for me this time.

I say, You don't like doughnuts much do you?

I'm celebrating, he says, as his finger hovers over the remaining seven, one by one, before settling on a glazed doughnut.

I say, How'd you know I'd be here?

A feeling, he says.

He wipes the corners of his mouth with a napkin.

I take it, he says, that you're accepting my offer?

SEVEN

Mr Police Officer barks something from behind his high-up mahogany desk, separated from the rest of the room in his glass cubicle.

I have no idea what he is saying.

He's looking at me, so I get up from the bench and walk up to the perspex box in the middle of the room.

He barks at me again.

I shrug my shoulders and I say, English. Do you speak English?

Mr Police Officer lifts his hand to his ear in the universal sign for *I can't hear you*.

So I shout, I don't speak Mandarin! Do you speak English?

He's pointing down at the bottom of the window, no idea why.

So I shout even louder, ENGLISH. DO YOU SPEAK ENGLISH?

At this point, the police station busy with cops and criminals is standing still, getting an eyeful of me and Mr Police Officer here.

I get back a load of eye rolling and some violent huffing, and he's now pointing like a madman to the bottom of the window, and I look to where he's pointing but I don't see anything except a little grey box.

Is this guy deaf?

I'm thinking what kind of idiot hires deaf police officers, and now the whole dumb situation is pissing me off, and Mia is pissing me off, and the stale, rancid air in this place has got me hot and sweating, and before I realize what's happening I'm yelling and swearing at this pig motherfucker in front of me, and I must be flailing around aggressively because now another Mr Police Officer is shoving my hands behind my back and I feel the cold shock of steel on my wrists.

And then this triad, he's tattooed all over, holding his shaved head where blood oozes from a dent made by a big blunt object, probably, comes up and points to a little button on the little grey box, which, now that I'm looking at it more closely, turns out to be some sort of intercom-speaker job.

Oh, nice one, I say.

The triad nods at me and goes back to his seat.

Original Mr Police Officer barks again, and then in the universal sign for *Fuck off, we'll deal with you later*, has me dragged away past my bench, past the old homeless guy, past the high-class hooker hugging herself.

* * *

Let's skip back a little bit.

Back in the doughnut shop, when Charles Hu says he takes it I'm going to accept his offer, I'm literally about to say, Why yes, I would love to accept your offer, when I feel a hand on my shoulder.

I look at this hand, then the arm it's attached to, then the shoulder, then the face, and it's a policeman in a blue shirt and cap.

Right next to him, is the nerdy young guy in the wheelchair and his girl that I, let's say, innocently hassled into leaving.

This lame couple are pointing at me and talking rapid fire, and next thing I know I'm being hauled up and out of my seat and shoved into a cop car.

How was I supposed to know he was disabled?

Now I'm on my way to a police station in a foreign country where I don't speak the language, *and* I left my camera on the table in the cafe.

No playing, how I'm reacting is I'm about to lose my

shit, on account of that camera (and the lens on it) costing thousands and thousands of pounds.

I say, Hey, did you pick up my camera in there?

The cops in front ignore me.

Fucking guy. Why didn't he just do what any normal man would do, sock me one in the face (or balls in this case, ha), bask in the glow of his girlfriend's adoration and be done with it?

Now I'm sitting on another bench, but this time it's in a cage.

I'm running through all the terrible scenarios that could happen.

Worst of them all, is I end up back in London.

No lie, I'm just not ready for that.

For sure I would be free and I could do whatever I felt like doing, but I would happily risk time in a Taipei prison for harassment if it meant I could carry on ignoring my old life.

After all, I was *the* master, Mia had told me, of ignoring things.

You seem pretty fine, she said, when I came home after getting fired from the paper.

I am fine, I said, opening the fridge.

She grabbed her jacket and said, Let's go.

The tall grass towered and glowed gold as we lay on the ground, staring up at the blue. I watched a cloud dawdle from right to left.

Mia moved to rest her head on my shoulder. Her hair tickled my arm.

For real, Mia had warmth. When I was with her, especially in the quiet moments like this, or after we had sex, I felt like I had warmth too.

Like I'd somehow absorbed it by being next to her, with her, inside her.

You know what it felt like? It felt like all the heavy, joy-sucking douchebag cynicism in me had vacated.

She rolled over and I rested my lips on the downy fuzz at the base of her neck, exposed by her tied-up hair.

My happy place.

I'm sorry you got fired, she said, turning her head towards me. For someone like you, that must be hard to take.

Someone like me?

You know. An overachiever. A perfectionist.

My hot breath bounced off her neck and back onto my mouth. I liked the way it made the fuzz stick to my lips.

I guess, I said.

Actually, I said, it makes me feel like trampled dog shit, replaying the still fresh, still terrible memory of my picture editor giving me the sack.

Mia shuffled her back and her butt into me more, took hold of my arm with her hand.

Love you, she said.

A metallic rattling sound shocks me out of my thoughts.

You, says Mr Police Officer, sheathing his baton. You go now.

He's looking at me different to the way he did before. Respectful like, the way he's holding the door open for me, waiting patiently, as though I wasn't the complete waster he previously thought I was.

What gives? I say.

The cell door clinks closed.

Someone save you.

In the corridor on the way out, I pass a girl struggling against the grip of another Mr Police Officer.

That movie star is the one you should be arresting, she screams. All I did was say no to him, she screams.

I put my jacket on and step out the police station. My face feels like it's being blasted with an array of high-powered hairdryers.

I take my jacket off.

I look around, and I have no clue where I am in this city. I look for a taxi rank, nothing. I scan the roads for cabs passing by, nothing.

A metro station it is.

Need a lift? says a familiar voice over my shoulder.

Charles Hu is waiting by the entrance of the station. Leaning against the wall of the building with his hands in his pockets. Smiling.

Come, the car is this way.

EIGHT

Right in front of me, is a giant building from a science fiction film.

Twisted glass and metal, bent into the shape of a double helix, with trees that look like they're growing all over its sides. It doesn't look like it should be able to stand up.

Charles hands me my camera. He must have picked it up after I got hauled out of the doughnut shop.

For true, the sight of it makes me weep with joy.

He says, Ready to work?

I say, Right now?

I feel the reassuring weight of the camera in my hands, the smooth action of the focus ring.

Sure, I say.

He starts walking. I follow. He goes around the building, stops at a big metal gate – one of those drop-down jobs – and swipes a little black disc at a pad on the wall.

The gate clunks open slow. We duck under and head inside.

The concrete ground slopes down for a bit, and when it levels off we're surrounded by gleaming, streamlined metal.

Rows of Ferraris, Lamborghinis, Maseratis, like a twelve-year-old boy's dream car collection. In the hands of rich, fully grown owners, it reeks of neediness.

Not like Charles here. When we got to his car, it was an old Audi from the eighties, its black exterior cleaned and polished like it was brand new off the factory floor. Inside was the same – pristine black leather and a cool alpine smell.

He'd taken a cassette tape from the glove box and put it into the deck as he drove us away from the police station – dreamy piano music cascading out of the car speakers.

Debussy, he said.

The car, the music, it was all exactly like him – perfectly understated.

We reach a door, which has another pad next to it on the wall. Through that, and we're in a lobby. Shiny, dark marble floors, big chandelier.

This building is no hotel – there's no reception desk – so I figure it must house a bunch of fancy apartments. To our left, a security desk, and beyond that, four lifts – two each on opposite walls.

The guard at the desk looks up from the little grey Mario running and jumping his way across the green screen of his Game Boy. Mario collects a mushroom, and I hear the rising arpeggio bleep as he gets bigger.

Good evening, Benny, says Charles.

Evening, sir, replies Benny, pausing his game, although there's no sign of recognition on his face.

He gives his attention back to Mario, and we walk towards the lifts. There's one with its doors already open, so we step in. Charles waves the black disc again and presses the top button. P is for Penthouse.

New security guard? I ask.

I don't know, says Charles. This is the first time I've been in the building.

I watch the numbers on the display climb.

Charles looks at the numbers too, clasping his hands in front of him. We don't say anything else.

When we get to floor 88, I feel the lift stop. The doors open onto a corridor.

A deep red carpet with a gold, floral pattern.

When we step out the lift, it's like we've just walked into space; there's no sound.

We walk towards the floor-to-ceiling window at the end of the corridor, passing a large oil painting on the wall. I stop to look at it.

One of those giant canvases, inside an elaborate golden

frame. An old-time admiral standing on the decks of a naval warship, posing with his chin up as his hand rests on the hilt of his sword. Corners of the mouth upturned in a sneer.

Charles has carried on walking without me, so I run to catch up with him.

We walk in silence for a little while. The window stretches further away, the walls warp and narrow.

I look down, stomp my feet on the carpet to figure out why I can't hear anything, and then smack my head on something hard.

The window.

Charles makes a left around the corner, and stops outside the first door we come to.

It's black, too heavy for an apartment door – more like the kind you'd find on one of those Victorian town houses in Kensington. It even has four rectangular panels, a gold lion for a knocker and a gold letter box.

88, says the number on the top of the door.

* * *

Inside, we stand in the dark for a moment. No one's in.

Charles flips the lights on, and the apartment sprawls. It's huge. For real, you could probably fit our flat four or five times inside it. Correction: Mia's flat.

Even though it's big, it feels . . .

Cramped.

And the air is like the air outside. Hot, damp, pushing down, down, down on us, from all directions.

Charles strolls through the space slow, eagerly sucking every minute detail of the place in through his eyes.

Open plan, sleek, shiny. The kind of place where the owner has no taste and no ideas and chucks wads of money at an interior designer to get them to deck it out for them. All the bells and whistles.

Charles walks up to the white sofa, one of those L-shaped ones, and lowers himself onto it. He puts his feet up on the matching footstool. He tilts his head back. His eyes are closed.

This is how my father used to look when he got back home from work.

It was usually late, around 9 or 10 pm. He'd come into the living room where I was watching a film on TV. *Demolition Man*. Or *Terminator 2*, maybe. My mother didn't really care what I watched, as long as I'd done my extra homework for the day. Nothing was more important than homework and full marks.

Man, that bit when Arnie gets lowered into the molten hot metal. That bit still haunts me.

My dad would drop his briefcase, loosen his tie, place his hand on the back of my neck for a couple seconds. Then he'd flop down next to me. Head back, breathing out slow, like he'd spent the whole day sucking in toxic fumes, holding it deep in his lungs, and was now exhaling it all out.

Who is this stranger? I thought. Drifting his way through life with a wife and a kid he only really saw at the weekends. Sometimes, barely even then.

I remember the sickly-sweet smell of his Brylcreem, left behind in the greasy dent of the sofa cushion next to my head, when he finally got up and plodded up the stairs to bed. This was when I was doing GCSEs.

Maybe that's when a few cells started growing weird in his body.

Charles gets up.

He says, Time to work.

He says, Here's your brief: I want you to shoot everything you see in this apartment – as if you were documenting it for a story.

I don't have my light meter or tripod on me, but using Sunny 16, I figure what with the abundance of light sources in here, I can get away with an aperture of 8, at 1/200th of a second. No blurry pictures.

I raise the camera to my face, and shoot.

I shoot the living room.

I shoot the roof garden.

I shoot the kitchen.

I shoot the dining area.

I shoot the cinema room.

I shoot the bathroom.

I shoot the five bedrooms and their en-suites.

I shoot a bunch of trophies in a cabinet.

In the master bedroom, Charles walks over to a chest of drawers and opens one up.

His fingers pick through the contents, and out comes some women's underwear.

Black, lacy, the kind bought from an expensive lingerie place. The kind bought to excite.

Then, what he does is he fishes out a matching bra and stockings, laying them all on the bed like he's leaving them out for someone to put on later.

At this point, I'm thinking this is kind of weird behaviour. I'm thinking, is he gonna strip off and put those panties on?

I'm thinking, do I even care?

To tell the truth, I'm excited by it. I can't even remember when I last felt like this, and it feels . . . *good*.

Like the last year I've been a brain-dead zombie, shuffling my way around an abandoned shopping centre.

But now – now I'm *alive*.

All I do, is I ask, Do you want to be in the shot?

No, says Charles. He says, Make sure you get a close-up of the lingerie.

I raise the camera to my face, and I shoot.

NINE

In this room, the light is red and low.

The vinegar smell of the stop bath bitch slaps my brain awake, on account of it being 2 am and I'm practically falling asleep.

In the tray in front of me, submerged under chemicals, I'm looking at a picture I shot earlier tonight.

The other thirty-five images from the roll are pegged to a line to drip dry – all of them shots of the apartment me and Charles Hu were just at.

This one in the tray, though. It's the last frame from the roll – a picture of Charles.

I know he told me he didn't want to be photographed. But this picture I took, he's got his arms crossed over his chest, staring at something on the wall.

If I remember right, it was a picture of this glamorous-looking couple. An Asian man, a white woman. They were at some sort of red-carpet event. A tuxedo and black tie for him, a sparkly gown for her. For sure they must be some kind of Taiwanese 'It-couple'. Around the shoulders of the man, the arm of another, older man, a slight distance away, face beaming.

The weird thing about this picture of Charles I've developed though, is how he looks. In person, he's all shot cuffs, easy smiles and sunbeams shooting out of his face.

In this photo of him, he's unrecognizable. His face is all tight. You can see his jaw busting out of his skin because he's clenching his teeth so hard. His eyes are all narrow. Dead eyes. And even though his clothes are sharp, the way he's standing makes them look like they don't fit right, like they're too big for him, like he bought them off the rail instead of getting them tailored on Savile Row.

Whatever he's looking at, it's messing with him something rotten.

I peg the picture of Charles next to the rest. No playing, this is just about the weirdest job I've ever had. And for sure, Charlie boy is into some freaky stuff.

But looking at the pictures I took, I know that I nailed the brief.

Doing good work and getting praise for it, that's gold right there.

I would bathe in praise if I could – fill a big bath full of the stuff, splash around in it like a happy little hippo.

For sure, I'll shoot whatever Charles wants me to shoot. I'll shoot him naked, spread out on a tiger skin rug in front of a roaring log fire, if he wants me to.

My phone chimes. A text from Mia, sitting under a stack of three other messages she's sent in the last few days:

Are you OK? Where are you? Haven't heard from you in a week now. Please let me know x

One kiss instead of the usual three. I half-think about replying. What I do instead though, is I bin the message.

While I'm at it, I delete her number from my contacts.

The pictures on the line now dry, I take them down, flip the lights off, and step out the 24-hour darkroom.

* * *

Walking down the street, I'm thinking I'm going to have some wild sex with Akemi when I get back to the hotel.

Maybe I'll get her to kneel down and throat my monkey first. Then get her to go on the bed on all fours while I plug her from behind. Maybe I'll finish on her stomach after a little while in missionary.

Through the front entrance of the hotel and into the lobby, I look for Akemi.

There she is, standing at the front desk, doing the night shift. Her hair's not in the usual bun. She has her blazer off, slight curves under a tight-fitting blouse, and for real, Little Sean is pretty much already at full hardness.

Hey, I say, approaching the desk.

She looks up at me for a second, before going back to the computer.

Hi, she says.

What are you doing? I say, leaning on the desk.

Working, she says.

I say, Fancy a little break? Maybe come up to my room for a bit?

She stops typing and looks up at me.

No, she says. I have work, she says.

And then she goes back to her stupid computer and the stupid click and clack of her stupid keyboard.

* * *

Back in my room, there's the smell of stale beer, teriyaki seasoning and sweat.

I kick the rubbish out the way to make the path of least resistance to the bed, and flop down, face first. So much for a ride with Akemi. What's with that girl, anyway?

I flip over onto my back and take my phone out my pocket. Let's see. I scroll through pictures of Mia.

Mia grinning outside the art gallery.

Mia making pancakes in her PJs.

Mia building some flat-pack furniture in our flat.

Nope. Good old internet porn it is. Maybe a hotel office scene featuring a hot concierge who seduces an unsuspecting guest.

I scrabble around for some tissues.

TEN

Picture a glass tank with glass so thick it's thicker than the wall of a house.

And in this tank, there's a perfect specimen of a tiger shark. Jaws hinged open bigger than your face, gums and teeth sticking out so far they look like they're going to slip out of its mouth.

Suspended, like it's floating in the air.

Black eyes staring right at you like any minute now it's going to come back to life, bust itself out of that tank, and when it does, it's going to eat you up like the tasty little treat you are.

And then just a few metres away from this crazy shark tank, close to the big white wall of the cavernous space, picture a wooden box with a double mattress on it.

There's a duvet and pillows on it, and the duvet's all crumpled up. The bedsheets are all coming untucked at the sides in big ruffles, and on the bedsheets there's brown sweat rings and old tights and dirty discarded pants.

Then on the floor next to this bed, picture a deep blue rug and a bedside table, littered with wrinkled tissues and condoms and cigarette butts and period-stained clothes and lube and pregnancy tests and empty vodka bottles and a stack of Polaroid pictures with a woman in shades smiling and, no playing, a little stuffed white dog.

This is the place Mia took me to our first time hanging out together – an art gallery.

You couldn't look at that bed and say that the artist had insane technical talent. Or even admire the dedication and hard work they'd put into becoming the best fucked-up bed maker in the world, better than all the other fucked-up bed makers out there.

But in a world where you had to be perfect, and clever, and tall, and handsome, and sporty, and musical, and excel at everything you did, all the time – here, well here were objects that were either ugly, or scary, or disgusting, or just straight up dead.

And behind these objects, there were people. People who took the messed-up things in their lives, and shame-lessly turned them into art.

Huge, ugly, beautiful pieces of art that sold for millions of pounds.

But that's not the point.

The point is, that confidence, that honesty – lying here on this hotel bed, in the dark, with the lightning bolt clarity you get after you shoot your load – I can for sure look back and say that's what had eighteen-year-old Sean hooked there in that art gallery.

And Mia? Mia was the one who opened up my eyes to all of that.

Eleven

This is me, watching a pile of clothes going round and round, round and round. Frothy water bubbling, washing machine humming.

This is me, sitting in an orange plastic bucket chair, in a row of five plastic bucket chairs, sandwiched between two aunties.

They smell like the sausage my *ama* used to make.

This is me, hanging out with the oldies under the yellow lights, between walls of washing machines and tumble dryers, with a bottle of Kaoliang in my hand.

This is me, face glowing, heart smashing, brain strobing.

I take my phone out my pocket. I poke the screen. Pokey poke poke.

Can't find Mia's message.

Right, right, right, I binned it – and her number.

New message it is then. Tap in the number which I remember like my date of birth.

Got into a car accident. In hospital but don't worry about me.

No kiss at the end, send. In my head, Sean dusts his hands off and pats himself on the back.

Another swig of Kaoliang is a swig of air, so I drop the bottle and it clunks and rolls on the floor. The old aunties don't even look up from their magazines.

Eyeballs on the screen, three dots appear under my message. She's typing.

Three dots disappear. She's thinking.

Eyeballs on the screen. Nothing.

Keypad. Tap in the digits.

Ring ring, ring ring.

Answer machine says, Hi, you've reached Mia. I can't pick up right now, but leave a message and I'll get back to you as soon as I can. Thanks! Answer machine beeps.

Hi, I say. So basically I got run over by a milk lorry. Not sure how long I'll be in hospital for.

I call again a minute later and I say, The doctors don't think I'll be able to walk again. I say, It's cool, I can be like Stephen Hawking.

A minute later I call and I say, Oh, while they were checking me out, they found a tumour. On my right arse cheek. They think it might be cancer. I say, No playing, just like my dad.

A minute after that, just as I'm about to hit call again, I get a text.

You're a prick when you're drunk.

I chuck my phone at the wall of whirring machines in front of me, where it smacks and clatters to the floor.

I immediately regret it and run to pick it up, checking I haven't broken it.

* * *

This is me, back in between the old aunties, swearing at my cracked phone screen.

Booze. Need more booze.

Hey, I say to the auntie on my right, got any booze?

The wizened old girl clicks her tongue and the look on her face reminds me of my mother when I drink in front of her.

You look ugly when you drink, my mum always says. She says, Your eyes go watery and your whole face is red. Then: Thank goodness you haven't got monolid eyes, a rounded head or a flat nose.

She's not wrong, I do look ugly when I drink. Which is why I don't drink all that much back home. But here, everyone looks ugly when they drink, so in that sense at least, I fit right in.

I pick up the empty bottle of Kaoliang on the floor and wave it in front of the auntie's face.

You know, booze. Alcohol. Speak English?

She shakes her head and buries her face back into the flimsy thin pages of her celebrity magazine.

I try the auntie on my left. No dice: this one is a champion ignorer, just like me.

I would run out and buy another bottle somewhere, but my clothes are still tumbling around inside that washer, getting nice and frothy, and I don't want anyone to steal them.

For real, leave any of your things unattended and they will get removed from your possession. Trust no one, Mr Mulder.

Not even old aunties who smell like the sausage your *ama* used to make.

Can't drink, can't sleep.

Can't get Mia out of my head.

Just then, I see a picture of a familiar-looking guy in the auntie's magazine.

No playing, it's the dude whose picture I caught Charles scowling at the other night in that apartment.

I tap the magazine a couple times and I say, Who is that?

Movie star, says the auntie, yanking her magazine away from my reach, giving me the side eye.

So you *do* speak English, you sly old bird.

TWELVE

Because of the effort, Charles takes off his jacket, then his tie.

He unbuttons his shirtsleeves and rolls them up. His forearms look lean and sinewy.

He rolls up the tie, and places it in his jacket pocket.

Spare, he says, carefully draping his jacket over the back of one of the plastic chairs like if he just tossed it, he'd launch a nuclear missile and blow up the world. Gentle gentle.

No jacket, no tie, still sharp. Especially with that bright white hair slicked back.

But then look at his feet, and you have instant clown. For real, not even Charles Hu can make those multi-coloured shoes look good.

A boom, a rumble, a crash. A whoop whoop whoop. High fives all round for the strike on the lane to our left.

The girl that just bowled pumps her fist, she's got on a red and yellow bowling shirt and one of those lame wrist supports.

Say cheese, I say, lifting my camera and taking a picture. She gives me a filthy look. Her identically dressed bowling sisters watch me for a second, deadpan.

Charles sits down and he says, I know what you're thinking.

A boom boom boom, a rumble rumble rumble, a crash crash crash. A round of bowling alley sounds on loop, mingled with ecstatic yelps and electronic music high on speed.

Let me hear it, then.

He says, You're thinking what on earth were we doing at that apartment the other night.

No, I tell him. I'm thinking I hate bowling and I hate bowling alleys.

He says, Westerners, you sure know how to suck the culture out of a place!

I think I've heard him wrong, so I say, What?

He says, Westerners, you sure know how to make things ace!

From out of nowhere, a ball comes flying from the right, lands on our lane and rolls into the gutter.

I look over, and a guy grimaces his apologies. Charles, he smiles and waves, it's okay, don't worry about it.

Say cheese, I say.

People starting off street photography get so worked up about how to take pictures of strangers without them noticing. Trying to figure out how to be incognito.

Truth is, you don't need to. Exhibit A: the picture I got of the pro-bowler girl. Exhibit B: the picture I got of the guy just now.

I'm not saying you won't look like a dick (you will), but you will probably never see that person again in your life.

But that's not the point.

The point is, you got your picture.

Charles tells me it's my go, nodding at the pins waiting at the end of the lane.

I say, Nah, you're good.

Mind if I go then? he says.

Charles lets the ball fly. To finish, his right leg shoots straight across the back of his left.

I always thought bowling was a dumb, fake sport for fat people with no coordination. Like darts. But looking at Charles here, well he makes the whole thing look slick. Even with the clown shoes.

Boom. Rumble. The ball looks like it's about to drop into the gutter, but right at the last second it curves back into the middle of the lane. *Crash.*

Charles's eyes have practically disappeared on account of the big grin on his face. He holds his hand up, I slap it. The man is giddy.

Isn't bowling great? he says.

If you say so.

My dad used to take me bowling every Saturday, he says.

Oh yeah? My dad used to beat me with a cane for not doing extra homework.

Ten more pins lower down. He asks me if I want a go now.

Go on, then, I say.

He says, Are you sure you don't want to put on some bowling shoes? They'll help with your approach.

I say, Nah, you're good.

I bowl. Correction: I let go. The ball drops, rolls real slow, and plops pathetic right there into the gutter.

This is why I hate bowling: I suck.

Too bad, says Charles as I sit down. Think of it as a practical joke.

My bowling?

No, he laughs. The apartment.

Oh. I love practical jokes, I say. Especially messy ones.

He tells me that him and this dude are old family friends carrying on their childhood games well into adulthood.

Last time, the guy bought an identical Audi to Charles's – same number plates and all – swapped them, and watched from a hiding spot in the garage as he spent an entire afternoon trying to figure out why he couldn't get into his car.

I massage my forearm, which is already tweaking with pain.

I say, He's going to flip when he sees the photos of his place.

Charles says, He certainly is. Did you manage to post them off to him?

I say, First thing this morning. He'll be looking at them and freaking out accordingly tomorrow.

Excellent, says Charles.

I say, Is he a movie star?

Charles says, He is.

He says, He's actually Chinese, from the mainland. Daniel Day-Lewis he is not, but he's not wooden and he is good-looking. Perfect movie star material.

Right then, a great hulk of a girl comes storming up to us, pointing at my camera. This She-Hulk is part of the bowling sisterhood on the lane next to ours.

She's saying she wants you to delete the picture of her friend, Charles translates.

Say cheese, I say.

She-Hulk stands there blinking. Her face goes all red, and she blows back to where she came from.

Exhibit C, ladies and gentlemen.

Only she's changed her mind, and now she's coming

back. Before I can lift my camera to fire off another shot, she's grabbed it and lobbed it over to where the restaurant is.

I watch in abject horror as it arcs in the air and thuds onto the ground in between two families sat down with their hotdogs.

You've got a lovely way with people, says Charles.

* * *

Back at the lane, and my camera is miraculously okay. Body undented, lens uncracked. Jeez, what a raging psycho bitch that girl was.

Thank god for carpet, that's what I say.

Charles is turning my camera around in his hands, giving it the once-over.

See, he says, engineered to perfection. Built like tanks these little Leicas.

I say to Charles, Your friend is going to think he's got a stalker, the way we got into his apartment like that.

He says, Or his wife's got a stalker.

Nice, I say. She's a movie star too, is she?

She is, he says.

Charles hands me back my camera. You know, he says, I still can't get over my luck bumping into you in that doughnut shop.

He says, Do you believe in fate?

I say, Not really, no.

I must say, he says, I was very impressed with the photos.

Picture Sean the happy little hippo, splashing around in the praise.

He stands back up again, holding his bowling ball up under his chin. Eyes focused on the pins.

He says, How about helping me with another practical joke?

I think about how being in that luxury apartment was a rush, for sure.

I think about how warm and fuzzy it felt to do good work.

I think about the coin I could get for doing another job.

And then I think about the morning after, and how the whole thing just felt more fucked-up in the hazy light of a Taipei day. A little too fucked-up.

I say, You know, I think I'm good.

Out the corner of my eye, at the far end of the alley, a figure stands still among the blur of bodies.

Face painted in swirls of red, white, gold, black.

Watching us.

I hear a voice calling out, *Guo lai!*

But when I turn to look proper, the figure is gone.

Ah, a shame indeed, says Charles, but I understand. He lets the ball fly.

IAN RUSSELL-HSIEH

Boom . . .
Rumble . . .
I watch the ball curl in the lane.
Crash.

THIRTEEN

She moves closer to Mia, gazes into her bottomless brown eyes.

She takes Mia in her arms, kisses her.

She holds Mia's hand, leads her to the bed, and they tumble down, down, down. A single mass of tangled up legs and arms and hands and lips.

Mia's infectious giggle, starting quiet, then getting louder, and louder, and louder.

Reverberating.

I wake up, alone.

And I know it was a dream, but for real, I feel like I've been played. Played like a chump by my girlfriend ... and her best friend?

How could she do that to me?

I don't know why, but for some reason it stings worse than if it was a dude.

* * *

Just as I'm about to walk out the hotel's revolving doors, I hear someone call my name.

I look and it's Akemi, standing behind the front desk.

There is no way I am falling for that again.

But instead of carrying on through to the street, I find myself turning around.

She says, I'm sorry I was rude to you the other day.

On my god, I say in mock horror, are you sure you can take your eyes off the computer? You might, you know, die or something.

She looks tired. She says, I was wondering if I could buy you dinner – to say sorry.

Ten minutes ago, I was raging at Mia for (fake) sleeping with her best mate, and for (truly) fucking up my life.

Here I am now, worrying if I should have shaved my patchy non-beard.

Okay, I say. I will accept your apology in the form of dinner.

She smiles (I don't think I've seen her smile before) and says, Great, meet me down here at six?

Six it is, I say.

* * *

One night back in January, me and Mia are walking through Soho, which then bleeds into Chinatown.

Short, old, wrinkly Chinese men and women in shabby clothes shuffle down the street around us. There's loads of them, like ants, coming in and out of the Chinese supermarkets, post offices and travel agents.

Scattered among these old folks are the younger Chinese – also loads of them. Pushing their glasses up with one finger, flicking the floppy hair from their eyes.

Laughing their awkward laughs, breathing visible air.

Why are they all so nerdy?

Mia says, What are those red banners with the calligraphy everywhere? Is it a New Year's thing?

Dunno, I shrug. Your guess is as good as mine.

* * *

Me and Akemi are walking through a night market.

Picture Chinatown in London, and then multiply it by a hundred.

There's more lights, more shops, more people, more noise, more smells, more people, more kitchens, more food, more people.

And not just old and young people like I'm used to seeing in Chinatown, but all the people in between too.

For true, this situation is not ideal.

Chinatown makes me uncomfortable just walking through it. Now I'm surrounded by the real thing, no coffee shops, no fast food joints, no corporate American chains, no nothing.

And I don't understand a word of what's going on.

Akemi asks me what I want to eat. Let's see. Between the stinky tofu that smells like actual shit, the slimy oyster omelettes, the giant fish heads stacked high and the pink octopus that's waving at me, no playing, I don't really feel like eating.

All around, alien food that looks like it's more likely to eat me than me it.

How about this place, says Akemi, pointing at a stall with plastic tables and chairs set out in front. The sign above is a big blue winking fish.

I say, Yeah, okay.

I don't eat seafood, have never eaten seafood. I eat like a little kid and my diet consists mainly of white foods like chips, and bread, and maybe the occasional chicken nugget.

Right here in front of me now though, is a huge bowl of yellow–brown liquid with what looks like intestines floating inside.

Inside the yellow–brown liquid of our bowl, a big black fish head pokes out the side like it's trying to jump on out of there.

If I take even one bite of this, I will be adding my own special liquid seasoning to the stew, soup, whatever it is.

Had this before? says Akemi, picking up a pair of red chopsticks.

Ha, I say. Have I had this before.

Want the eye? she says.

Do I want the eye, I say.

I say, Of course I want the eye. That's the best bit.

Right now, all I can think about is my *agong*'s face folding in on itself when he realized I didn't speak Taiwanese.

My parents shrugging their shoulders like, *What can we do*?

Right now, I'm wishing I took more interest when my parents tried to introduce me to their food.

I'm wishing I didn't quit Chinese school on Sundays after one day so I could go and play footie with the white boys in my neighbourhood.

I'm wishing I was a kid who inhaled goddamn fish eyes like they were Chomps, Curly Wurlys and Push Pops.

Akemi says, Are you okay?

Right now, I don't want to feel like a failure in front of this girl, so what I do is I grab me some chopsticks (I can use those, at least), pluck out the eye from the fish head and put it in my mouth.

Mmm, delicious, I say.

My favourite part of the fish, I say.

The doughy, chalky eye squishes between my teeth, explodes all over the right side of my mouth.

It doesn't even taste of anything, really, but the thick texture makes me want to hurl.

A little bit of puke comes up, but I swallow it back down along with the eye.

And now there's a thick, fish eye coating all over the back of my tongue, and I can't get rid of it.

Don't they put water on the tables here?

For sure, I will never eat another stinking fish eye, ever again.

Have the other one if you want, says Akemi, smiling.

And like an idiot, I pluck the other eye out and put it in my mouth.

FOURTEEN

For the second time since I've been here, I'm doubled over.

Puking my guts out.

My diaphragm aches with the effort, my throat burns as the acid ejects.

The fish head intestine stew didn't spend too much time in my stomach, but I did chug a lot of it, so there's little chunks of it splattered all over this guy's shop stall.

All over his neat display of purses and handbags.

The river of night market punters slows to investigate, giggling and crowding forward to get me on video. Hey, good for you guys.

The stall owner is talking at me, but Taiwanese people sound angry all the time, even when they're not, so I can't tell if he's actually pissed off. Me? I'd be shitting rusty nails if some kid came and barfed all over my absorbent, un-wipeable, home-made goods.

I can't help but laugh. This is what happens when you pretend to like things you don't like.

What's he saying, I ask Akemi, blocking a sick belch with my fist.

You don't know? she says.

I steady myself on the stall, shake my head.

I swear you spoke Mandarin when we first met, she says.

I shake my head again.

He's worried about you, she says, checking you're okay.

And I say, I am not okay. My insides and throat feel like they are on fire.

The guy disappears and comes back with a glass of water and a towel. I drink, and the ice cubes make a nice clinking sound and the cold water makes me feel better.

Shit, I'm sorry about your stall, I say, looking at the mess I made.

He repeats a phrase twice and waves his hand – *Don't worry about it.*

For real, I say, I'll pay for all this stuff, just tell me how much.

The phrase comes out again and he hands me a T-shirt from the back wall of the stall – a spot I managed to miss. I look down at my fishy, pukey clothes.

Cheers, I say.

* * *

Another food stall, another plastic table. Akemi is smiling at me.

You look like a real tourist now, she says, admiring the pink T-shirt that says *I <3 TP* on the chest.

It's two sizes too small for me, so my belly pops out from the bottom like a little piggy.

Please, I say. No more seafood.

She hands me a hot, steaming golden bar wrapped in a paper towel.

I look over her shoulder at the kitchen she got it from, and there's a long queue of people snaking down the street, waiting to get their orders in.

Try it, she says. You'll like it.

I sniff it, and it seems harmless enough, so I bite, and I crunch, and I burn my tongue, but then I get to smooth, sweet ice cream on the inside.

It's nice, I say.

See? she says.

I'm not getting any of that Antarctic chill that usually comes off this girl back in the hotel. She's more smiley, for one. And without the hotel uniform she almost looks relaxed.

You know, making me sick is a funny way of saying sorry.

You were acting like you loved fish eyes, she says. Maybe you should have just been honest.

No lie, the girl is right.

This ice cream definitely makes up for it, I say. You are forgiven.

How come you don't speak Chinese? Or Taiwanese?

I swallow the last of the deep-fried ice cream. Any chance of another one of these?

FIFTEEN

The second Ed bent down to pick up this nice fat conker he'd found on the muddy floor, I heard this *shhhhhhhhrk* sound.

Yeah, he'd split his trousers right where his crack was, bright red pants showing through the ragged, gaping hole.

And this voice, from the top of the Dell, it says, Oh shit. Look at what Ed Wet The Bed just did!

Ed and me look up, and it's Lawrence, pointing down at us. Hillard comes out from behind a tree and sniggers his little rat snigger through his little rat teeth.

Dude, says Ed, clamping both hands onto his arse and straightening up. Can you pick up my glasses?

He sniffs a goopy string of snot back into his nostril.

He says, Seriously, I wish my mum could just buy me a uniform that fit for once.

I go and pick up the glasses, half-buried in a pile of

orange leaves, and wipe the muddy lenses on my sleeve. I put them back on his face, careful to make sure the arms hook around behind his ears.

I say, Sorry dude, that's the cleanest I could get them.

The snot string is dangling back down out of his nostril again, so I get my hanky out and hold it against his nose while he blows.

At this point, Lawrence and Hillard have slid down the slopes of the Dell to squeeze a bit more entertainment in before we have maths.

What's the matter, Ed Wet The Bed, Daddy-Waddy not make enough to buy you clothes that fit? says Lawrence.

And then he turns to me and he pulls his eyes into tiny slits and he says, Is it nippy out here or what?

Hillard thinks this is the funniest thing in the history of the world, and starts chopping the air, making kung fu noises.

I hope you haven't brought any of that chinky food in for lunch, says Lawrence. You stink the whole school out when you eat that slop. Disgusting.

I know you won't believe it, but at this point I didn't know what to do or say.

Right then, I just wanted a ham sandwich, some Dairylea triangles and a packet of salt and vinegar crisps, like every other kid in school.

Lawrence and Hillard got bored waiting for a reaction

from me and Ed, so they climbed back up the steep slopes and went looking for other kids to torture.

No playing, I wish I'd just socked Lawrence one right in the nose and smashed it into a million tiny pieces.

All I did, I picked up the shiny conker that Ed had spotted, and said, Here you go dude.

He said, Dude, I gotta keep my hands over my arse crack. Can you look after it for me?

Sixteen

Charles Hu inserts a small, thin, wooden stick in between his teeth. He manoeuvres it up, pulls it out, reinserts it, manoeuvres it up again.

Ah, there you are, he says, inspecting the smudge of yellow food speared on the end of the toothpick. Revolving it around like it's a diamond or something.

He puts the stick back into his mouth and sucks.

The kissing-teeth sound he makes, this is exactly the sound my dad used to make after every meal.

I took a pack of his toothpicks to school one time, got one out after lunch and started digging around inside my mouth. Kissing my teeth – just like my dad. For real, I didn't even have anything caught up in there.

My friends thought I looked mint as. Mr Mills told me to stop it immediately and watch my manners young man or there would be lines to write.

Looking at Charles examining the food that's caught in

between his teeth and swallowing it back down, I'll admit, it is kinda disgusting. No lie, Taiwanese aren't so hot on their manners.

Charles's place is real similar to that apartment we got into the other night. It's in a big, tall building made out of steel and glass. There's a fancy lobby area, six lifts servicing the building, long, winding corridors.

The apartment itself is huge, too. Bigger than the movie star's place. An eight-bedroom mini-mansion at the top of a skyscraper, with a frigging rooftop garden wrapped around it.

A hundred per cent, Charles Hu is living The Dream.

Where the movie star's place was decorated in your generic, no-personality way, Charles's apartment is all intricately carved, dark wooden screens, floor-to-ceiling calligraphy scrolls, hyper-sized paper lantern lighting and Chinese sculpture.

Old, but modern in its own way.

I say, What do you do again?

He says, Oh, you know. He eyeballs a freshly impaled bit of chewed-up food. A bit of this, a bit of that.

Looks like you really lucked out, I say.

He puts the toothpick back into his mouth, eyes narrowing. Make no mistake, he says, the little wooden stick wagging up and down, I've had to work very hard to get to where I am today.

Hey, I say, hands up. I'm sorry, I didn't mean to offend.

Charles's eyes go back to normal. He says, It's okay. A lot of people assume my family was rich. But we were as poor as they came, he says. My father worked on building sites six days a week, seven if he could.

My dad, he worked hard too, I say.

Charles says, He got cancer in the end. Never spent the time to look after himself. When he died, my mother had to find whatever work she could to support us. Washing restaurant and hotel linen, cleaning at the local school. You name it, she did it.

My dad, he died of cancer too, I say.

Charles says nothing, and in the silence, I hear chants and shouts coming through the open window.

We go outside, onto the roof terrace. Down below, a pulsing dark mass marches through the streets. Pops of colour from the placards and the banners, but from this height, there's no reading the words on them.

I say, What's that about?

Charles, he's looking down, a slight smile on his face. He says, Protesters. They're not happy about the trade deal with China.

We watch for a little while as the bodies move along the street, as the shouts fade away.

Back inside, I see a bunch of pictures in frames on a

sideboard. I pick one up of a little girl and a woman, both of them grinning at the beach.

I say, This is your wife and daughter?

Charles says, Are you thirsty? How about some fresh *dou jiang*?

I think I know what that is. Soy milk. My parents loved it. Me? I never tried it. And no playing, milk can't be as bad as fish head stew.

So I put the picture back down and I say, Yeah, I'd love some.

* * *

Whiz whiz whir are the sounds coming out of Charles Hu's mouth.

Once he kills the blender, he says, Apologies, this thing is much too loud. What I said was, have you ever tried fresh, home-made *dou jiang*?

I say, I've never even tried old, ready-made *dou jiang*.

Shaking his head, he pours the white liquid into a cloth-covered saucepan, and then, squishing it through with his hands, he says, The secret is to heat it up slowly.

After the milk's been heated up, the two of us just watching the stuff bubble, he chucks a handful of ice cubes into two glasses and fills them up.

Here. You'll love it, he says, offering me one of the glasses with a glint in his eye.

I sip. It's sweet and it's nice, but then comes the after-taste on the back of my tongue, which is weird.

Ugh, I say, putting the glass down, wiping my mouth on my sleeve. Not for me.

I think I see Charles's face tighten, but it comes and goes so fast I'm probably imagining it.

You're so English, he laughs.

For true, he wields that phrase like a weapon. Just like my parents.

Seventeen

I close the door of Charles's bathroom and lock it.

While I piss, I feel the heat radiate through my cheeks thanks to Charles's last words.

And for the first time since I've been here, I miss Mia.

I'm on the verge of tears and everything, having a slash in some billionaire's toilet on the other side of the world.

Pathetic.

Okay.

I have for sure not been all that great to Mia in the last year. I can see that now. I might even go so far as to say that I have been a dickhead of extreme proportions.

But in my defence.

Picture being hot shit at everything you do, all the time.

You can watch people go about their day, doing the same things you do, only worse. And you can tell them, Great job, or, you smashed it, and make them feel nice, but deep down, when you get to the real truth, you know that you're better than them.

And there's the love, too. The admiration, the back-patting, the big ups. No playing, people love you when you're good at things. They might not even say it, but you can tell just by the look in their eyes how impressed they are by you.

I zip up my trousers, wipe the rim of the toilet, and flush.

As I wash my hands, I avoid looking at my reflection in the mirror.

Where were we? So you're hot shit. Now picture getting sacked one day for screwing up a job in the most basic way.

Your boss is telling you how useless you are, how much of a hindrance you are, and now he's got to pull some miracle out the bag to get the job done.

Because you suck.

And in the process of you getting fired, and then in the days, and weeks, and months, and even year after, you're thinking that maybe you're not as good as you are at the thing you thought you were really excellent at.

And you're getting this image – of sweaty Tom and his angry, despairing face telling you that your pictures are rubbish – invading your thoughts at random times in the day, every day.

And maybe you don't want to get up in the morning anymore, or have a shower, or tidy the flat, or go out, or speak to friends, or go out with your girlfriend, or do anything. Except play video games and watch porn.

I'm not trying to make excuses, but, well, yeah.

And thinking about it, Mia didn't look at me, disappointed, when I told her I got fired from the paper. She didn't love me any less.

She just ... loved me. Because I was me.

Eighteen

I'm walking back to the hotel to pack my stuff up. In the morning, it's time to fly back home.

After rain, the night air is fresh – the first time since I arrived that it hasn't pressed on my skin and invaded my nostrils and lungs.

It's a relief. And with the relief, comes some kind of un-smogging of my brain.

Here's what I know:

I have no clue what I'm doing out here, really.

I have been a shit boyfriend, and I need to fix things with Mia. Apologizing would probably be a good start.

I think I have just dodged me a massive bullet by not agreeing to do another job for Charles. Whatever is going on between him and the movie star, it's not just friendly banter between two old pals.

To be fair, he didn't hold it against me. He even gave

me this expensive bottle of whisky to take home with me, wishing me safe travels.

This place feels less alien already, though. I'm even finding the girls here cute, which would never have happened before.

And look, this girl walking towards me is super cute in her blue miniskirt and black knee-high socks, and as we pass, we turn our heads to smile at each other, she's got these mad contacts that make her eyes look huge, it's a little interaction that makes me feel pretty good, and then there's a loud, blaring *HONK* in my left ear, and a car has just screeched to a stop literally fifteen centimetres away from me, the guy at the wheel bashing on the horn, *honk, honk, honk*, he's screaming at me, so I step back onto the pavement as fast as I can, and off he zooms down the street in his ninja-silent Toyota Prius.

I look at the stream of people behind me, but the girl is gone.

* * *

Just across the street from the hotel, just minutes before nine.

There's Akemi, coming out the revolving doors, putting on her jacket.

I shout out her name, but she doesn't hear me. So I start running—

—And then the world flips upside down.

I'm in the air.

I'm tumbling over something hard.

And then I'm right-way round again, and I can feel the cold, hard ground on my cheek.

And my hand is kind of hurting, so I lift it to my eyes, and I see that there's blood all over it.

And in front of me I see red taillights, glowing in exhaust smoke. The bottle of whisky Charles gave me, it's smashed into little shards all over the ground.

And above the lights, a cartoon picture of a smiling cow, a tall glass of milk in its hoof.

And I hear a voice, close and then far, call out, *Guo lai!*

Seductive and singing and sly.

And a little giggle gurgles its way out of my mouth, before everything goes dark.

NINETEEN

In the corner of the living room, there was a CD player.

Naaamooooo aaaaaaaamiiiiiituooooofoooooooo . . .

Naaamooooo aaaaaaaamiiiiiituooooofoooooooo . . .

Naaamooooo aaaaaaaamiiiiiituooooofoooooooo . . .

The monk drone from its speakers went on and on, all day and all night.

And my dad, well he was lying on his back in the middle of the room, raised up.

And me and my mum, we're on our knees side by side.

The sick-sweet smoke from the joss sticks swirling, snaking.

My throat is scratchy from all the chanting.

I'm a fifteen-year-old kid with no idea what I'm doing. I mean, I know *what* I'm doing, I just don't know *why* I'm doing it in the place I sneakily play *Street Fighter* in the middle of the night.

My parents don't pray, they don't meditate. I go to a Church of England school, and this is all like some sort of mystical nightmare.

My mum, she's crying and her chanting's all broken and choked.

Me, I should be eyes forward, but I can't look at my dad. I just can't.

The closed eyes.

The tight, white skin.

The way he seems to have shrunk.

Because I feel like if I look any more my mind will actually
                    break.

And it's scary, that body lying still up there.

It sure as hell isn't my dad anymore and for true I am fucking scared.

All I can do, is chant.

Naaamooooo aaaaaaaamiiiiiituooofoooooooo ...

It goes on like this for days.

TWENTY

My dad says, Come here, son.

And I get up from the chair, walk the two steps towards his bed.

He waves me in closer, closer.

I lean down, smell the fragrance-free soap on his neck mingled with the bitter, antiseptic stench of the hospital room.

He hugs me, hugs me tight. And even though it's the first time he's ever *really* hugged me, I know it's tighter than he ever would have hugged me back when he was healthy.

When he finally lets go, I see sadness in his eyes.

I smile at him, give his tiny arm a squeeze.

And then I leave, relieved.

* * *

I wake up, alone.

When I open my eyes, at first I think I'm in my dad's hospital room.

That terrible TCP smell, along with something sour. Sterile lights above me on the ceiling. Ugly hospital curtains.

But then my brain un-fuzzes a bit and I realize that would be impossible.

My left leg is sore, so I look down and see that it's in a cast.

I check my hands, and they're not broken.

I check the rest of me, and I am sore all over, but most of the soreness is in my leg, so I think I am generally okay.

And then I remember that image I saw before I blacked out on the road – the smiling cartoon cow with a glass of milk in its hoof.

One of life's sick jokes.

My phone is on the bedside table. The screen is even more cracked, but it still works.

And I didn't have my camera on me, so it's still at the hotel – talk about good luck. (Good luck may be a stretch when you've just been run over, but I am alive and I think I have just dodged me a massive bullet.)

New message to Mia:

Actually got hit by a milk lorry, no joke. Am OK but I've broken my left leg. In hospital now.

An instant message back:

Do you ever take anything seriously?

I think about this for a second.

I'm pretty sure you told me I took things too seriously.

And then I add:

You sound a bit confused, if you ask me.

And I feel her tossing her phone and walking away, 6,000 miles to my left.

TWENTY-ONE

Wow, you look awful, says Akemi, sitting next to my bed.

Really awful.

And I say, I feel pretty awful. I feel like I have been hit really hard by a milk lorry.

She says, Actually, it was just a van.

She tells me the doctor told her I was very lucky not to have sustained further injuries, that if the van driver had been going just a couple miles faster I could easily have ended up with two broken legs, or broken ribs, or broken arms, or a broken neck, or punctured lungs, or head trauma leading to loss of speech and memory and the ability to eat, or I could have tetraplegia, or quadriplegia, or I could be in a deep coma right now and never wake up ever – or all of the above.

She tells me the van driver was reading a message on his phone, and didn't see me until he'd felt something like a cow hit his van. She tells me he'd already been involved in another road accident a few months ago – where the guy he hit *did* end up in a coma, woke up FUBAR and had to kiss his wife and two kids bye bye – and that it was outrageous that this piece of trash was still allowed to be on the road behind the wheel, that if she was in charge she'd have stripped away his driver's licence, banned him from driving for life and put him in prison for a long, long time.

The more I hear, the more I feel like some sort of miracle has happened.

I think back to the bowling alley and when Charles Hu asked me if I believed in fate – if I was destined to meet him in the doughnut shop.

If I was destined to survive getting squished by a milk van pretty much intact.

If I was, in fact, destined to be dumped by Mia.

I say to Akemi, When can I get out of here?

And she says, They just need to keep you for another night, and then you can be discharged.

She says, You'll need someone to be with you for a while, until your leg's healed up properly. I've got to work, but I talked to my dad and he said you could stay at his place.

He's a bit intense, she says, but he's got a nice place at least.

I spent the last of my money on the flight back home,

and I rinsed my scrawny savings coming out here, so I am, essentially, flat broke. That means no more hotel, and I don't want to ask Charles, because, well, that's obvious.

So I'm thinking how staying with Akemi's dad might be a good idea. It would give me some time to get my head straight before I talk to Mia properly, too.

I say, that's really kind, thanks.

And then I say, Peeing feels weird when you're in bed and you don't have to take your trousers off and you've got a tube stuck up your thing.

And then my bladder empties, and empties, and empties, and it's the only thing in my body that feels good right now.

Twenty-Two

The next morning, and even though I've only been in hospital for a day and two nights, I feel like I've been here for infinity.

Breakfast was on a par with aeroplane food (I hate aeroplane food), and I am desperate, gagging, to get out of here, because I also hate hospitals.

I hate the smell, I hate the sickness, I hate the pain, I hate the way I get images of my dying dad when I'm in them, the memory of sitting on the steps outside the building, hugging my knees, crying, after he finally went.

When Akemi comes in, bang on visiting time, I say, Can we go now?

And she tells me yes, there's just some final paperwork to be done, that her dad will be here any minute to pick us up.

And I lie back in my bed and smile, because the

painkiller is now kicking in (liquid morphine is *good*), and coupled with this excellent news I am feeling warm, and cosy, and for true I am so, so grateful and happy to have Akemi here looking after me that I am about to burst with happiness and joy, rainbows-shooting-out-of-me-with-unicorns-sliding-down-them vibes know what I mean?

Then Akemi, looking at the door, she says, Here he is. Let's get you dressed and then we can get out of here.

I look over, and closing the door behind him, smiling a big smile, is Charles Hu.

He says, Fancy meeting you here.

And I think that, surely, the universe is fucking with me.

TWENTY-THREE

There, says Charles. How's that?

I lean back in the armchair and stare out the wall of glass in front of me, the city spreading out hundreds of metres below like an oil slick. Layers of faded hills in the distance.

The hospital sent me away without any drugs, so all I'm on right now is your regular paracetamol and ibuprofen, but it's pointless, because the lightning bolts striking up and down my leg are teeth-grinding agony.

I say, I'd be better if they'd given me some proper painkillers.

Charles, he looks at my fat, casted leg raised up on the footstool, and he says, Painkillers are for the weak. If you can control your mind, you can control the pain.

I laugh, and I think I am not in the mood for this Eastern hocus pocus crap right now.

I say, What is this, some kind of Shaolin monk shit?

You westerners, he says. You've lost touch with your bodies.

He tells me to close my eyes, and to focus on the pain.

And I say, The goal is to take the pain away, remember?

He tells me to close my eyes, and to focus on the pain. To visualize it.

So I sigh, and I do it.

I zero in on my leg, a limb in the darkness. I float through the skin so I can see the muscle and the sinew and the bone, and I see the pain as lasers zooming through it, Boba Fett shooting all hell up in there with his blaster, and the blasts get faster, and faster, so fast that they combine into one blinding light, expanding and exploding until my whole leg is engulfed.

Eyes still closed, I say to Charles, This is dumb. I have never been in more pain than I am right now.

Then Charles tells me to let the image of the pain go, to think of a place, or a moment in time that makes me happy.

So I do it.

I scrub the light bomb from my mind, make it go all dark.

I bring up a picture of a room, flooded with golden hour light – the kind of light photographers' wet dreams are made of.

White curtains billow in the gentle summer breeze.

Outside the window, I can see trees full of green leaves, branches swaying, like a scene from a Terrence Malick film.

I'm lying on my side, and in front of me I can see Mia. She's got her back turned to me.

We're in bed, naked, and she's got her hair tied up in a bun, exposing the soft skin of her neck.

I move in close, rest my lips on the base of her neck, breathe in the smell of her coconut shampoo.

The pain in my leg, it's sort of gone, more like a dull ache now.

Then I remember where I am, and that I've probably lost Mia for good.

Charles says, How's the pain?

Unbearable, I say.

Twenty-Four

For true, life in a wheelchair one hundred per cent sucks.

Basic things like getting in and out of bed, or going to the toilet, or washing – not so basic anymore.

Akemi got this special cast protector for me, which helps. It slips over my leg and seals itself like magic so it doesn't get wet when I'm in the tub. I've still got to rest my leg on the edge of the bath though, and it hurts like a motherfucker.

Then there's things like cooking for yourself. I can't even reach the kitchen counter to prep food, so Charles is cooking all my meals. Of course he is a kick-arse chef – he's cooked me *niu rou mian, zong zi* and hotpot so far – and the salt, sweet, fat and heat of these crazy-smelling dishes is overwhelming.

Like I've unlocked some sort of secret level of taste on

my tongue, and now there's no going back because I've seen the other side. (The dishes all have 'umami', according to Charles.)

And I think that Akemi was probably messing with me making me eat that fish head stew, but now that I've upgraded my taste buds, I think I'd even find that dish tasty too.

Gourmet Taiwanese food aside, needing someone to do things for you all the time, it's like you're a useless hunk of meat and no playing, that isn't the one.

Charles's place is all on one level, so that's something at least.

Deed done, I wipe my arse, use my arms to push myself up and into my wheelchair, and flush the toilet.

I notice a brown bottle of something on the counter – it says *post poo drops* on the label. I have never seen anything like this before, so I unscrew the pipette, squeeze the rubber top, and drip some drops into the toilet. Orangey. I squeeze some extra drops in just because, and then put the bottle back on the counter.

Like the rest of the penthouse, this bathroom is immaculate and shiny. The marble surfaces are mirrors, the toilet is limescale-free, even in the cavernous shower space there's no mould.

It looks like the room is brand new, but Charles tells me he's lived here for years. I haven't seen a cleaner around, so the only reason it's this spotless, is because he's cleaning it himself.

I've seen this kind of thing before in my mum – Charles is a certified clean freak. Like one of those OCD people you see who clock a speck of dust on a surface and have to wet wipe it away, otherwise they will die and the world will explode.

I see some pills next to the sink as I wash my hands, but the label is in Chinese, so there's no figuring out what they're for.

Hands dried on the plushest towels I've ever felt on my skin, I wheel myself into the living room, where I find Charles stood in front of the penthouse's IMAX-sized windows.

He's flowing graceful and slow, through what looks like a series of tai chi movements, dressed in a white tee and some sweats.

I think of my dad, who never gave a shit about exercise until the day he got his cancer diagnosis.

After that, it was tai chi in the morning (because growing and harnessing his life force would kill the cancer, naturally), long strolls in the woods, breathing deep in through the nose, out through the mouth, in through the nose, out through the mouth, every single day until he couldn't.

I'd go with him on his walks sometimes, and the

swinging of his arms, the bounce in his step, the pointing at trilling birds in the trees, the singing – it felt for a minute like all this fresh air was going to get him better.

But the frailness, it bugged me.

It bugged me that he didn't spend the time to get physically strong before all this shit happened.

It bugged me that the only real time I got to spend with him was when he was sick and I never got the best of him.

Too little, too late.

Charles Hu catches my eye as he pivots his body in my direction, arms sweeping low and then up like he's painting the air.

Good morning, he says, lowering his arms and standing straight.

He says, Breakfast?

* * *

The table is loaded with food, tea, coffee and OJ. Pastries, croissants, toast, jams, cereals, cold meats, it's like a five-star hotel breakfast buffet (what I think that might look like, anyway), and there's also a bunch of unfamiliar foods.

Charles points at each of these dishes one by one: Here we have *cong you bing jia dan, mantou, xiao long bao, you tiao*, and, your favourite: freshly made *dou jiang*. We've got sweet *dou jiang*, we've got salty *dou jiang*, and we've got my personal favourite, *dou jiang* with peanuts.

Me, I'm ready to roll, to see what new flavours are going to noodle my mind, but I start off easy and grab the thing that looks most familiar – the dough stick studded with spring onion that my mum used to get in from the street stall when we'd visit my grandparents – and the bite is crisp, hot, salty, oily and delicious.

Charles bites into a dumpling and slurps the soup inside, and we spend a minute or two munching in silence.

I know what you're thinking, says Charles.

You're thinking that night in the apartment was a little . . . unsavoury.

I mean, you could put it that way, I say.

You're thinking you don't want to be involved with a strange man you barely know and his perverted jokes, he says.

I mean, you could put it that way, I say.

You're thinking life is too short, you nearly died, and you'd rather spend your precious time salvaging what's left of your relationship with your girlfriend.

I mean, you could definitely put it that way, I say.

And then he takes a sip of his soy milk, crunches on the peanuts, pauses for a bit.

And he says, I haven't been entirely truthful with you.

He says, Let me explain.

Twenty-Five

Picture a young Charles Hu, fifteen years old.

He's just walked the five miles home from school in some old, beat-up sandals handed down through five brothers. This house, it's in the middle of nowhere, surrounded by acres of scrubland. And this scrubland, it's in Yunlin County, right in the middle of the west coast of Taiwan.

And instead of going inside the house to get a snack, or play games with his brothers and sisters or the neighbourhood kids (there are no neighbourhood kids because there is no neighbourhood), he walks around the house and straight into the ramshackle hut at the back – which is also where he sleeps, on account of there being eight kids in total and there not being enough room for him inside the two-bedroom, single-storey house.

He lights a candle because there's no electricity (there's no plumbing, either), and sits down. He flips open a textbook he'd managed to borrow from a kid who lives miles down the dirt track, a kid who is now studying economics at National Taipei University – a regular miracle for round these parts.

And young Charles, he moves the candle closer to the pages, and he gets to studying mathematics.

Because the Hus are broke. A drought messed up the farm that's been in the family for generations, and his father's now working for shit-all money in construction, building the country's first ever motorway.

Because the only way he's going to help his folks out is to study, graduate at the top of his class, get a scholarship to university and get rich.

Charles's daddy, he's always talking about his boss, looks up to him something crazy.

How distinguished he is in his Savile Row suits, tailor-made on visits to London.

How he only smokes imported Nat Sherman cigarettes with gold filter tips.

How civilized he is with his good manners and easy charm.

How he says the west is the future – America is investing heavily in the country, and one day, well one day Taiwan will be a major, global player. Just like America.

And young Charles, just like his daddy, well he thinks this all sounds magical.

He'd love to go to America. And so he studies.

* * *

One night, at around midnight, young Charles's mother and father walk into the hut.

Charles, he looks up, and he sees their faces. Worried-looking.

And his father, he says to Charles, Son, we've got some bad news.

He says, We went to the hospital in Chiayi earlier. The coughing and the breathlessness ... it's because I've got lung cancer.

Lung cancer, thinks Charles. This is what his *aku* died of a few years ago.

His father, he says, Don't worry, they caught it early.

And young Charles, he closes his textbook.

He listens to the roar of the cicadas outside.

He's freaking out, because what is he going to do without his dad?

The man who taught him how to fish, how to swim. The man who would take him to the market, just the two of them, and secretly buy him a big plate of sweet *xueha bing* loaded with mango and condensed milk.

105

He fights back the water in his eyes. And quiet and calm, Charles says, What can we do?

Charles's father, he sits down next to his son, his face lit up by the flickering candle. He says, There's treatment I can have, radiotherapy, chemotherapy, maybe even surgery.

And young Charles, he says, Where are we going to get the money from?

His daddy puts his arm around him, draws him in close.

His daddy says, I work hard. My boss can help, don't you worry about it.

His daddy squeezes him, and he says, Okay?

Twenty-Six

Charles stops talking, and the dishes on the table are all empty, on account of me having eaten everything off them while he was telling me his story.

He gets up from his seat, starts stacking the plates and the cutlery and the glasses.

And I say, Hold up. You can't just start clearing dishes. Did your dad's boss give him the money for his treatment or no?

At the sink, Charles is rinsing the plates off, one by one, before placing them carefully in the dishwasher.

He's got his back to me, but between the hunched shoulders and the hanging head, it's pretty obvious the story for young Charles doesn't end well, just like the story for young Sean.

He tells me that even though his dad was the hardest-working man on the crew (he worked extra shifts to help out, never slacked once), his boss – the rich man who flaunted his wealth and adoration for all things west – refused to help him with his treatment.

Because if he helped Charles's daddy out, he would be setting a precedent, and would have to help all his workers out – even though doing that would have been a cinch.

Because he had his own wife and kid to look after, and what with keeping her in the newest designer dresses, overseas private school fees, piano and tennis lessons for the boy, as well as staff for the house and the pool and the gardens and the stables, annual ski holidays in Courchevel *plus* maintenance and upkeep of his new super yacht, it was already killing him as it was.

While he's telling me all this, Charles is transforming into the Charles I photographed back in the movie star's apartment – that tight-faced, glazed-eyed man I don't recognize.

Charles, he sits back down at the table and pours me another coffee, then fills his own cup. He's loosened up now, back to his normal self. Watching the steam dance in the air.

He says, The movie star. The movie star is my father's boss's son.

And I go, Jesus Christ. Well that's all starting to make sense then.

He apologizes for not telling me the truth before, and that he understands if I don't want to help him.

Because, truly, he wants to make the movie star's life miserable.

Because the movie star is the boss's greatest achievement. His life, his world, his everything.

Because destroying the golden son while the father watches? That is sweet, sweet revenge.

Because, truly, he'll never be able to sleep, or get rid of the all-consuming rage that pulses through his veins all day, every day, until the scales are finally balanced.

I think about what young Charles had to go through losing his daddy.

And I think about what I had to go through.

Having to see my dad scared, ashamed and embarrassed because he was losing clumps from what was once a full and thick head of hair: for true one of his biggest fears made real.

Having to resort to a wig that was constantly fussed over, that made him look more pathetic and weak than it did well.

My phone chimes. A message from Mia:

No. You're the one that's confused.

TWENTY-SEVEN

Please, says the movie star, on his knees, looking up at the woman in the red dress.

I can't do this anymore. It was okay when we were on set, I could handle it. But now? It's killing me.

Akemi blows musky smoke into the dark, and it swirls, lit up in the light, caught in between the flickering projector and the giant screen.

She points and says, I don't get it. This guy is such a bad actor. Why is he so famous?

I take the nearly finished joint from her, feel the warmth of it on my fingertips. One last deep toke, the red glows brighter in the dark of Charles's private cinema room, and it's done.

I feel myself fill up with the smoke, hold it in as long as I can.

I finally exhale, and after a coughing fit that has me

doubled up in my seat, I straighten up and say, Looks count for a lot. And that actor's pretty good-looking. For an Asian guy, anyway.

She glances at me. What's that supposed to mean?

Tell me one Asian guy who is better looking than George Clooney.

She looks at me, tells me she can think of dozens. No, more.

And then she adds, You realize you're Asian, right?

And I say, Am I?

* * *

The opening credits roll for a new film.

Opening shot over some plinky-plonk orchestral music: Mia, in a kitchen. It's an old black and white film.

She's wearing an apron over a dress, fifties housewife style, preparing a meal while the movie star sits at the dining table, reading a newspaper. It's so big it covers his face and his body.

The camera zooms in on the hob Mia is cooking on: a big bubbling pot of water, another of gently simmering, clear brown broth.

She drops some noodles into the water to cook, and shouts to the movie star in an old-timey American accent, Dinner will be ready in just a tick, honey!

We see Mia drain the noodles. She places them into a deep bowl, she ladles the broth over, she sprinkles some chopped spring onions on top.

She brings it over to the table, where I'm now sitting, the movie star to my left. He bends the top corner of his paper down and grins at me a grin full of perfect, white teeth.

The movie star folds his newspaper up, puts it down on the table next to the steaming bowl, and breathes the fragrance of the dish in deep.

He says, Sweetie pie, you've simply outdone yourself, this looks and smells absolutely delicious!

Mia, she just stands there with her hand on his shoulder, admiring him.

And then he devours the food like he's some sort of rabid wolf. He's got the bowl in his hands, boiling soup pouring and splashing all over his face, noodles on his crisp white shirt and tie, noodles on his perfectly pressed trousers, noodles frigging everywhere.

Mia, she just laughs as if this is the most adorable thing she's ever seen.

Me, I'm horrified by the display.

From beyond the glare of the studio lights, the audience laughs.

And Mia, she smiles a glowing smile at him, then takes her apron off and sits down to my right.

And while the movie star carries on shovelling the

noodles into his mouth with his hands, she turns to me, still smiling, puts her hand on my leg, and she says, You're the one that's confused.

And the camera pans out and moves high above me as I stare straight into the lens, while the audience's applause crescendos.

* * *

Akemi sits down again and the lights fade back on.

I say, Where did you get that weed from? I think it is fucking with my head.

And she says, A friend of mine grows his own stuff. Good, right?

I fidget in my wheelchair, try to get comfortable. No dice.

My dad, she says, nodding to the screen. He's a big fan of that actor – has been ever since his first movie. I remember him taking me and my mother to the cinema whenever there was a new film of his out. I never got the appeal, personally, but I'd look at him in the movie theatre and he would be engrossed the whole way through. One time, we finished one screening, and stayed in the theatre to watch the thing all over again.

I say nothing, just wait for her to fill the silence, because I'm pretty sure Charles does not want anyone knowing what the story behind him and the movie star is – or the stuff we got up to together.

How did you meet my dad, anyway?

I look around Charles's cinema room, the deep red of the plush seats, the uplighters on the dark grey walls giving off a soft, yellow glow. In here, our words leave our mouths, hit the fabric-coated walls and die a quick death.

I tell her we bumped into each other at a doughnut shop, the day after I arrived in the city.

I tell her it was lucky, considering I had no idea what I was doing here.

She does this scoff and says, What a crazy coincidence. My dad, he would call it fate. Did he call it fate?

He did, I say.

And now that I know her and Charles are related, I take the opportunity to look at her in this new light, to see what other similarities I can find.

The eyes, they're bright like Charles's, for sure, with an intensity that could be mistaken for outright hostility if you didn't know any better.

And they have the same nose.

So what, are you working with him now? she says.

And I say, I only did one job for him.

And she says, Doing what?

And I say, Photographing stuff.

Just as well, she says. My dad, he's into some shady stuff.

She says, Want my advice? Don't get too involved. And if you do, I don't want anything to do with you.

She leans further back into her seat, looks around the room.

This place, she says. It's ridiculous. He thinks money is the answer to everything.

I tell her, Well yeah, it pretty much is.

And she says, Even love?

I think about Mia, and I say, Love will kick you in the balls the second it sees an opening.

Try telling that to my mother, says Akemi. I think she would have preferred his love over his money. I think I would have preferred his love over his money.

Where's she at then, your mum?

Back home, in Japan.

And her face tells me that's the end of the conversation, so I don't say anything more.

Twenty-Eight

There's a Taiwanese soap opera that is so cheesy you wouldn't believe.

Soft, dreamy visuals over slow piano ballads where the characters swoon and cry and laugh and *yearn*. My days, I've never seen so much yearning in my life.

I came across it when I was flicking through the channels one time, bored out of my mind. Pretty cringe, but before I moved on to the next channel, the lead female character's stepmum was wanting to pimp her out to some sleazebag to feed her alcohol addiction, then the lead-male character finds out he has a frigging tumour on his brain, but if they operate he has a slim chance of survival, so it's either die quick or die slow, and now I am hooked because I want to find out if the two leads make it in the end.

* * *

I stare out the wall of glass in the penthouse's living room.

I attach my telephoto lens onto my camera, aim it at the neighbouring buildings, and watch people getting on with their lives out there.

Who knows, maybe I'll watch a murder going down, and me and Akemi can solve the mystery, figure out what happened.

In the building in front, I see a young mother and a baby, tickling and giggling. Some days the baby is crying and although I can't hear it, from the looks of its mother it's loud, it's been going on for hours.

On the floor above, a shirtless dude practising *wing chun* on a wooden dummy. Sweating with the effort.

In the next building along, a woman sitting at her desk in front of the window, one minute furiously tapping at her laptop with a smile on her face, the next, she's staring out the window, looking like she's thinking about what she's going to eat for dinner.

In the apartment below hers, a young couple, around my and Mia's age. I watch them cook, eat, watch TV, fight, fuck, laugh, dance, read books, throw parties.

I used to love watching these two at first, but after a little while it just made me think of Mia, how our lives were kind of like their lives.

And looking at this couple down the barrel of my lens, it just compressed everything, shoved my old life right into

117

my new, Mia-less existence's face, like the way telephoto lenses make the sun look huge, way huger and way closer to the mountains than it really is, so I pretty much avoid that window now.

* * *

What I do, is I walk.

Give me my camera, and I will strap the thing around my neck, and walk for hours and hours.

Miles and miles.

No playing, I'll walk from eight in the morning until twelve at night. Sometimes even later.

Because unlike a painter, or a writer, or even a studio photographer, I can't just think of an image in my head and make it appear.

I have to walk to find it.

I don't even know what I'm looking for most of the time. I just walk, and watch.

Everyday life in London.

I walk and I watch, in the moment. And if I see people doing things that speak to me, I just follow my gut and shoot. Get in as close as I can.

Because if you're not in there with them, you're detached from the scene. There's no intimacy to the frame.

Sometimes I get home from a day of shooting without firing off even one shot.

It's not the easiest way to make art, I'll give you that.

But it's the only way I know. And the feeling when you've had a good day? When you've tapped into some next-level plane of consciousness, and everywhere you go there is an intriguing, surprising picture to be made, overflowing with the emotion, the humanity, the soul?

For true, there is nothing like it. I live for that feeling.

It's weeks since I went street shooting, and I am suffocating.

* * *

Charles beckons me over to the kitchen table and says, I've got something to show you.

I wheel myself over.

In his hands is a tablet. He pokes the screen a few times, then lifts it to show me.

I take the tablet. No playing, what I'm looking at is a grid of pictures – a picture for every room in the movie star's apartment. In the living room, I see the movie star gazing at himself in a giant mirror. Smiling.

I say, When did you install cameras in that place?

He says, When you were photographing it.

Street photography is one thing. (I mean, it *is* legal in

a bunch of countries to take pictures of people in public without them knowing. And for sure, you've been filmed on CCTV hundreds of times a day.)

But spy cameras in someone's home?

I look at the movie star again, still smiling at himself in the mirror.

I say, Isn't this illegal or something?

Charles, he leans back, sips his tea, and says, It is.

And his conviction is so strong, so unwavering, that I am completely swept away in it.

* * *

I lie back on my bed, tablet in my hand.

No lie, this is an unexpected blessing – one more thing I can do while I wait for this stupid cast to come off my leg.

I scan the screen for the movie star, but he's nowhere to be found. The wife though, I see her walk into the living room, something rolled up under her arm.

She's got her long, blonde hair tied up in a ponytail, she's dressed in a vest and tight leggings.

She unrolls the thing she's holding onto the ground, and starts stretching.

Long limbs, a curvature that urges.

It's weeks since I had sex.

My monkey wakes up and goes, OOK, and here it is,

another welcome escape from the mind-numbing monotony of my existence.

* * *

The movie star is sat down at the dining table.

The wife places a plate in front of him and sits down in the chair opposite.

The movie star has a mouthful, chews, and swallows.

He puts his fork down, says something to his wife.

She looks at him, says something back.

He gets up, walks over to her, and pushes her off her chair and onto the ground.

He points his finger at her, shouts at her.

* * *

You look tired, says Charles.

Did you get any sleep last night?

I look up from the tablet and I say, Not really, no.

He says, You've been watching those two all day and all night for a week.

He gently removes the tablet from my hands and he says, Maybe I should take that now.

* * *

I am recovering in a luxury penthouse, but I don't care what anyone says, a prison is a prison.

I spend my days watching soap operas, watching the neighbours, watching the movie star and his wife (now only when Charles is with me, though).

I always think about calling Mia. I want to talk to her about us, but chicken out because it's just too much.

What would happen if she told me that was it?

That I'd messed up too bad and there was no way back?

I don't know if I could handle it.

But now? At this point, I don't give a fuck. I just want to go home and get her back.

I take painkillers that don't work.

I brush my teeth, wash my face.

I shimmy into bed, lie awake in the dark for hours, fall asleep fully aware of not wanting to move my leg and hurt it more, and dream of weird things that I try to remember the next morning, but can't.

No playing, I don't know how much more of this I can take.

* * *

Week five, and I think I have gone insane.

Twenty-Nine

Ed says, Dude.

I say, Dude.

He says, Where have you been?

I say, I'm in Taipei.

He says, Why are you in Taipei?

I say, I don't really know.

He says, Poppy saw Mia yesterday.

I say, Oh yeah? I was just thinking about calling her. Mia, not Poppy.

He says, So ... Poppy told me about this Tanner guy.

He says, She doesn't think much of him. One of those city boys with more cheddar than soul, know what I mean? Reckons you and Mia are way better together.

And I say, What now?

THIRTY

Hi, Sean. How are you?

I'm not gonna lie, I could be better.

Ed told me you're in Taipei.

Uh-huh.

That you actually did break your leg getting hit by a milk van.

Yep.

Sorry I didn't believe you.

That's okay. I get why.

I always wanted to go with you to Taiwan, remember? But you never wanted to.

Yeah, well maybe you can go with Tanner.

. . .

Ed told you?

Ed told me.

So you're just going to dive in, no small talk?

Yep.

I fucked up, okay? I'll admit it. I'm sorry. You shouldn't have found out about Tanner that way.

You think?

I should have told you that night on my birthday. I was a coward. But you have to understand, you changed – ever since you lost your job. You just retreated into yourself. I tried, but I couldn't do anything to help you. And you wouldn't admit that you were depressed, so no one else could help you either.

. . .

Do you know what it was like? It was like being with a ghost. And I didn't want to be with a ghost. Ghosts are cold.

. . .

I'm not making excuses, what I did was wrong. But there were reasons for doing what I did. Can you at least see that?

. . .

[What I want to say, is, Sure, I can see that, and I'm sorry for being such a rubbish boyfriend for the last year or so.

What I want to say, is, I was in a really bad place. All I ever do, every waking second of my life, is try to be the best at everything. Because it's the only way I feel good about myself. I got fired, felt like a failure, and was probably depressed. No, for sure depressed. I should have listened to you. Will you forgive me?

What I want to say, is, I love you. I just want to fix it. I don't care about Tanner. I just want to fix us.

Instead, what comes out is:]

What kind of a stupid name is Tanner, anyway? I bet his dick is bigger than mine, isn't it? I bet the sex is better too, isn't it? Why did you go out with me in the first place? You could have done so much better.

Goodbye, Sean. I hope your leg gets better soon.

THIRTY-ONE

Fuck.

THIRTY-TWO

Whatever marker pen the guy used was already running out, so the banner reading *CUTS HURT* in big red letters was faded. You had to really focus on it for a few seconds to make out the words – probably not what the guy underneath holding it wanted.

He looked beat up without being beat up. Pale with dark patches under his eyes. Like a panda.

But even though he looked like shit, you could tell he was mad – little globules of spit coming out of his mouth, frozen in time.

Here's Tom, sweat leaping off his forehead like lemmings, splashing onto the photo of the angry panda teacher he's eyeballing from a distance of two inches.

Can somebody, he says, straightening up, get the bloody air conditioning fixed? It's hotter than my arsehole after a chicken vindaloo.

Around us, the paper's staffers carry on. Keyboards tap, telephones trill, shouts shoot across the office from opposite sides.

Everyone hustling.

Fucking air conditioning, says Tom. You'd think one of the nation's biggest broadsheets could at least keep its staff from melting.

For real, it wasn't actually that hot.

Sean, says Tom. This teacher here, he's out of focus.

I knew he was right, but hoped it wasn't so bad that he'd notice.

He points to the other pictures spread out on the table. He says, This one's out of focus, this one's out of focus, they're *all* out of focus. How can we show this strike if all the bloody pictures are bloody blurry?

There's no point in having sharp images when you have fuzzy ideas, I say.

You're not Jean-Luc Godard, says Tom. And this is journalism, not art.

Me, I'm looking around the office. I catch Michael's eye as he looks up from his computer. His eyes widen and his mouth spreads to the bottom corners of his face.

Michael is the only other East Asian in the office, and I spend my days resenting him, resenting his presence.

Because the two of us working here among these white people means we get lumped together. But Michael is a try-hard plonker, it's embarrassing, and for true, I don't want to be lumped in with him.

I am nothing like him.

I'm not gonna lie though, the sympathy kind of makes me feel better. He is a dick, but even dick sympathy can make you feel grateful when you've fallen into a deep pile of shit with no way to climb out.

They're not that soft, I say, picking up a fuzzy picture of a police officer pinning a woman down to the ground. In her hand is a placard saying ... Nope, I can't make it out.

Wait. *FAIR PENSIONS FOR ALL*. That's what it says.

What a fucking disaster, says Tom, leaning on the table, looking at me sideways.

The veins in his temple pulse a Morse code at me.

He says, We can't use any of these.

He sighs, and puts the end of his pen in his mouth and chews.

At this point, I have no idea what to do. So I just stand there, watching him.

Jane!

The volume of his bark makes me jump clean out of my skin.

See what Reuters have got on this public sector strike. We need pictures to go with Michael's copy, ASAP.

Jane looks hassled as hell, but nods and gets busy on her computer.

Jesus Christ, says Tom. This is the third assignment in a row where you've come back with substandard pictures.

No playing, I was drowning. My first big gig as a photojournalist and I'd fumbled my way through assignment after assignment.

Not enough coverage, pictures filed late, soft, out-of-focus frames.

Global readership plus millions of eyeballs equals big pressure, you know?

Tom here had seen something in me, taken a chance, and I'd proven him completely, utterly wrong.

He says, Sean, you've got an incredible eye. The way you capture emotional stories in one single frame is remarkable.

I mean that, he says.

But maybe a local paper might be more suitable for you right now, he says.

I'm thinking, A local paper? Fuck that.

I say, Tom, please. Next assignment, every picture will be tack sharp.

He says, Sorry, Sean.

He collects my shitty, spread-out photographs into a neat pile, taps them against the glass table to get them nice and neat, and then hands them over to me.

I take them from him, I don't even look him in the eye. Partly due to how pissed off I am, mostly due to how ashamed I feel for having done such a terrible job for the guy.

My guts were turning, my ears burning.

I'd never been fired from a job in my life.

I'd never been shit at anything in my life. I know this, because I have actively spent my life avoiding anything I've sucked at.

This. This is what happens when you go out of your comfort zone. You get sacked.

On the way out the office, my stupid stack of photographs in my hand, I pass Michael's desk. He gives me the same look again.

I tell him he looks like a retarded pug and that he can stuff his stupid, ugly face up his puckered arsehole.

THIRTY-THREE

The day before I get my cast off, and I've just finished watching my new favourite soap opera. (The male lead found out that the female lead's stepmum was pimping her out and flushed all her alcohol down the toilet! And then he whisked the female lead off and away! We're only mid-season though, so I haven't got my hopes up.)

Next on the Sean-stuck-in-an-apartment-with-a-broken-leg itinerary: checking in on the neighbours.

I get comfy in the chair I've set up on the terrace specifically for this activity (I've got a nice side table so I can put a drink on it and everything), and I pick up my camera.

There's the young mother and baby, tickling and giggling.

There's the guy practising *wing chun* on his wooden dummy.

There's the woman who's normally sitting at her desk, tapping away at her computer. Sure enough, she's typing.

Wait, now she's reading what she's written, and now she's stood up with the laptop in her hands and – oh, she's smashing the laptop onto her desk, over and over and over again. It looks like she's screaming (although it's hard to say, her hair's covering most of her face). Now she's dropped the obliterated computer and is slumped on the desk with her head in her arms. Yikes.

The young couple, they're nowhere to be seen, which is a shame, because now Mia has lobbed a grenade onto our relationship, I weirdly want to watch a happy, functioning couple go about their lives together.

I carry on moving the lens to the left across the building, and pick a random window with someone inside it.

This one'll do.

It's a guy, he looks like he's twenty, twenty-one. He's sat at a desk, reading a book. I can't make out what the book is, so I zoom in some more, and see that it's called *Tales of the Grotesque and Arabesque*. One of those old-looking books, bound in worn leather, the title embossed in gold.

I aim my lens back at the guy to see what kind of person reads this sort of ancient literature.

His face is out of focus, so I dial the image in a bit more.

And the guy, well the guy looks like me.

Thirty-Four

When I say the guy in the window looks like me, he's not just an Asian guy with similar features.

He actually looks like me.

(Or do I look like him?)

He's got the same tattoo as me, running down his right forearm.

He's got the same small scar at the corner of his left eye.

(The way I got that – my mum was having a screaming fight with my dad at dinner. I was only eight, but I'm pretty sure it was something to do with a woman he worked with. At any rate, she threw her chopstick at him, it missed, hit the oven door, broke in two, ricocheted and hit me right in the face. They both looked at me for a few seconds, and when I didn't cry or anything, they went back to their argument.)

He's even got the same haircut as me.

Is this the guy Akemi thought I was, back when I first met her in the hotel dining room?

Through the lens, he's still, focusing on the story he's reading. No expression on his face.

I zoom out a little, focus on the room he's in to see if I can get any more information on this guy.

But the room he's in is blank. White walls with no pictures. No furniture, apart from the simple desk he's sitting at, and an Anglepoise lamp on that.

Now that I look at him more closely, the stillness on him is next level.

He's not just physically still (apart from when he turns a page, obviously). It's like he knows something that the rest of us don't.

Like he knows he's supposed to be in that room, reading that book, taking up the space he's taking up in there.

I'm watching him for three hours, just looking through my viewfinder.

He hasn't stood up to go to the toilet, to get something to eat or drink.

He's just sat there, totally focused on his book.

Before I know it, it's getting dark. I'm only noticing because he reaches out to turn the lamp on.

The light acts as a spotlight, bathing him in golden light while everything else around him – the other windows in the building, the people inside those windows – fades away.

Taking pictures of naked girls again? says a voice right by my ear.

It scares the shit out of me and I nearly fall out of my chair. I look around, and it's Akemi, squinting, trying to see what it is I'm observing so studiously.

I half-think about getting her to look through my camera at the guy over there in that building, but then realize that would be an awful, awful idea.

I smile and I say, What else am I supposed to do with this dud leg?

She makes her scoffing sound, and she says, Have fun, Mr Peeping Tom.

When she steps through the sliding window back into the penthouse, I lift the camera back up to my eye.

But when I eventually find the window again, it's dark.

THIRTY-FIVE

The next morning, the first thing I do when I wake up is head out onto the terrace so I can see what Other Me is doing.

For some reason I can't find his window.

When I do finally manage to find it, the blinds are open, but there's just the chair and the desk and the lamp. The book is there, too, propped up against the lamp.

I pan right and I pan left to check the windows either side, but there are other people in those, so they must be different apartments I'm looking into.

All I want to do right now is watch that window, get another glimpse of this guy, but today is the day I get my cast off.

For weeks, all I wanted was to get this stupid thing off my leg. Now the day finally comes, I'd rather sit out here and stare at a window.

No lie, I'd even take the horrendous itch under there that I'm not allowed to scratch, to be able to sit here all day.

But Akemi and Charles come out to take me to the hospital, and there is nothing I can do about it.

* * *

How does it feel to have your leg back?

Charles is at the kitchen counter, putting the kettle on to boil.

Me, I'm sitting at the table, desperate to go out there to see if Other Me is in his room again – and if he is, whether he's doing anything other than reading his book.

Yeah, it's a relief, I say, as Charles places a cup of green tea down in front of me.

He sits down next to me, sips his tea. Now that you're fully recovered, I suppose you'll be heading back home?

I think about Mia, and how Mia is, ugh, Tanner's now.

I think about my joblessness and my high level of broke-ness.

I think about my homelessness.

And I say, Actually, I was thinking about staying here and maybe doing some more work with you. If that was okay by you, of course.

He raises an eyebrow. What about your girlfriend?

Yeah, I say, burning my tongue on the tea. I don't think that's gonna work out, unfortunately.

Ah, he says, that is a shame. I'm sorry to hear that.

Yeah, I say. It is what it is, I guess.

Well, as they say, her loss is my gain, he says, smiling his wide smile and clinking his cup against mine.

* * *

This time, I have my tripod set up, on account of me wanting hard evidence that this other me out there is real, and not some figment of my fucked-up, cabin-fevered existence over the last six weeks or so.

Like, see-it-with-your-eyes-on-photographic-paper-you-can-hold-up-to-your-face-and-examine type of evidence. With a magnifying glass, if you have to.

The thing with telephoto lenses, is they are big. Really big. So if you attach one to your camera, you have to use a tripod to make sure you don't get any blurry shots – especially with low light and slow shutter speeds. If you have a tripod, you should really use a shutter-release cable too, just to minimize any shake from pressing the shutter button.

I look in the direction of the window, and again, it takes me a while to find.

When I do, he's there.

I get a smack of adrenaline, just like when I'm on the street and I capture a stranger's image when I'm a metre from their face.

It's the same as yesterday, he's sat at his desk, reading his book, with the lamp on. Still as anything.

I press the shutter release, wind the film on, press the shutter release, wind the film on.

And I sit back in the chair, and I watch the silhouette in the window, and I fall asleep.

THIRTY-SIX

I wake up, alone.

My leg feels small, and light.

It feels cold.

It feels like it can breathe.

I open my eyes, and I'm outside, in my recliner, on the terrace of the penthouse, on account of me falling asleep at my stakeout spot.

I yawn a wide yawn, look through my camera. But he's not in his room right now.

And then I remember that I'm not an invalid anymore, that I can actually walk now, that I can get out onto those streets down there.

* * *

This is me, munching on some *you tiao*, a few doors down from the building's entrance.

Waiting for him to come out.

It's 6:30 am on Tuesday, so if I'm on my game, I should be able to catch him walking out the door on his way to work.

If he works, that is.

The building itself is nothing special. An off-white block on a street of off-white blocks.

Scooters buzz drunkenly up and down the street.

Above, a lady is hanging her washing out to dry on her balcony railings.

I guess Taipei is like London in that way: multimillion-pound projects plonked right in front of your old, run-down buildings.

This is me, munching, keeping an eye on the door. I've been here ten minutes or so, and no one has come out yet.

This is me, munching, realizing that I should maybe disguise myself a little – so that if he does come out and see me, he won't, you know, freak out and have a heart attack or something.

Just your regular dude, hanging out on the street, eating his breakfast.

But what if he comes out the building when I go off to buy my disguise?

I weigh the dilemma up in my head for a minute, and decide it'd be better if he didn't realize what was going on.

On my way here, I passed a shop that sold cheap

baseball caps and sunglasses. The owner was just sliding the shutters up, so I go back and buy a plain black cap and some Wayfarer knockoffs, and I put them on. Inconspicuous like.

Just as I'm about to get to my waiting spot, I see that he's right there at the front of his building, leaning against one of the tiled columns.

Reading his book.

The plan was to follow him around a bit. See what he gets up to in his day.

But this guy, he doesn't seem to do anything apart from read that book. And by the looks of things, he's going to be there for a while, standing comfortable there in that morning slice of warm, golden light as the city wakes up around him.

I watch him for a few minutes.

Now that I can see his body fully, the rest of our physical similarities come fast. He's the same height, he's the same build.

But even so, he seems to take up more space than I do.

And even though you can't see it, you can sense this invisible forcefield around him, and it gives him this power, this authority.

At this rate, I could be standing here all day.

So I walk up to him.

And I say, That looks like an interesting book.

THIRTY-SEVEN

Me and Erin, we used to take it in turns to go around each other's houses after college. This was when we were around sixteen.

Erin was this blonde-haired, blue-eyed metalhead, with pale white skin, who was constantly twirling her hair round and round, round and round.

The first day we met she was slacking off in art class, doodling on a piece of paper and rocking backwards and forwards on her chair, while Mr Hallam was talking to us about composition in photography and the golden mean.

When I turned to see what this penduluming thing in my peripheral vision three desks down was, I was smacked in the face with a scrunched-up piece of paper.

The face on me must have been funny, because she was creasing up silently.

Outside, she told me she was sick of her mum and dad fighting all the time.

I told her my dad had cancer.

We'd hang out in our bedrooms, listen to music, watch films.

Spend hours snogging, nothing else. Partly because at least one of our parents was always at home, and partly because I'd never had sex before, and to be honest I'd never even had this kind of thing with a girl before.

I was just amazed she didn't find me and my slanted eyes ugly.

One afternoon, this was in the summer, just as we were about to finish our first year of college, we're outside the main building and she says, Hey, my parents are out tonight. Wanna come round?

And I say, Sure.

We ride the bus to her house, and at this point we've been going out for a few months already, so we've got into a kind of easy rhythm.

She opens the front door, I kick off my shoes, and we go up to her bedroom.

Same as usual.

But after we make out to a soundtrack of Incubus for a little bit, she reaches down my body and grabs my dick, a first for us.

And instead of fist pumping the air and shouting in my

head, *GET IN THERE MY SON*, all I can think of is this article I read in *Loaded* magazine, illustrated with a bar chart and everything, that ranked guys' penis lengths by race.

And how the men with the smallest dicks in the world were Asian men.

And I'm thinking, Shit, what if she pulls my trousers and my boxers down and sees what's under there and laughs?

What if she says, Is that it? So what they say about Asian guys is right, after all.

I'm thinking, How am I ever going to be able to live up to this girl's expectations?

I'm also thinking, What if I jizz too quick, and all over her duvet and her sheets – how are we gonna clean that up?

And before I know it, I've lost my wood. Erin pulls back to look at me.

She says, What's wrong?

And I say, Nothing. Absolutely nothing is wrong. Everything is fine, I am having an amazing time.

She says, Then why aren't you hard anymore?

And I say, I think I'm just tired. Do you wanna make out some more?

She says, Let's just listen to the music, and she cranks up the volume on the stereo before lying down with her hands behind her head.

Cold as a motherfucker, this one.

I think about lying down, squeezing next to her on the single bed, but she looks pissed off, so I just sit there at the end of the bed, listening to an angry song about how it's nice to know you.

And that is the last time we hang out in her bedroom, or my bedroom, because a couple days later she tells me she doesn't think it's working, and I am dumped for Gaz, the knob who wears chunky silver chains around his neck and wrists, and drives a white fucking Vauxhall Nova.

THIRTY-EIGHT

This? he says, turning the book around to look at the cover. Yeah, it is good.

There's a story in it, he says, about a dude and his doppelgänger – which I really like.

Even his voice and accent are exactly like mine.

Although the delivery – it's more assured.

I say, A doppelgänger? Like a double?

He says, Exactly.

He gestures for me to sit down on the steps next to him, which I do.

In this story, he says, confident and measured, there's a kid called William, way back when in England, who meets another boy at school. And this boy, he's got the same name, the same appearance, he's even born on the same date.

I whistle in disbelief, because *what the fuck?*

He says, Crazy, right? So this boy tries giving William some advice, but William isn't going to take any of that. Anyway, William goes to university, gets into sketchy shit like cheating at cards, hooking up with married women. That kind of thing.

But each time, his doppelgänger stops him from doing the thing, just as he's about to do it.

I say, That's got to be pretty frustrating for William. What happens?

Well, our William gets so mad, he drags his doppelgänger into a room and stabs him to death.

While he's telling me this story, Other Me is looking at my face, and even though I've got a cap and sunglasses on, I'm feeling like maybe the disguise isn't enough.

He says, Do I know you from somewhere? You look kind of familiar.

I say, I don't think so. I've only been here for a couple of months, and most of that I spent cooped up in an apartment with a broken leg.

Yikes, he says. That must have driven you nuts.

Then his eyes light up and he snaps his fingers: Got it! That actor, Takeshi Kaneshiro. That's who you remind me of.

This is something my mother said to me one time when I was a kid.

Very handsome, she said.

But then I googled this actor, and saw that I looked nothing like him.

Other Me, he says, It's hard to say with those sunglasses on, though. Why don't you take them off?

I'm thinking, How the hell do I get out of this one then?

And then I think, Fuck it.

So I take off my sunglasses, and wait for the incredulous reaction from Other Me as he realizes we're practically the same person.

Yep, he says. Takeshi Kaneshiro. Definitely.

You know, he says, some people say I look like him too?

THIRTY-NINE

Was that any good? says the blond guy with the big jaw.

He lowers the sheet of paper, looking at us with wide, grey eyes.

In the middle of this studio space he got me to rent out for the day, Charles is sat down on a stool. He says, Will you excuse us for a minute?

Sure, the guy says, and steps outside.

Charles says, What do you think?

Me, I can't focus on what we're doing. On account of my encounter with the other me this morning.

I'm shook.

It felt like the whole conversation he was alluding to the fact that we're the same, without explicitly saying it.

Charles is looking at me expectantly, so I shake it off and I say, He was pretty good. Maybe the best we've had all day.

Charles goes to the door to take a look at the guy again. I like that he's American, he says. Tall and muscular. Handsome, too.

He looks like Brad Pitt is what it is, I say. A regular Adonis.

I bask in the guy's presence, even though he's not in the room anymore.

A feeling of half-admiration, half-self-loathing.

Tall, good-looking white dudes, they have that effect on me.

Charles folds his arms and looks at me. Is he making too much of it, though? Is he overdoing it with the hand gestures and the tears?

Why don't we give him some pointers and let him have another go at it?

Good idea, says Charles.

* * *

Adonis composes himself, clears his throat.

He's standing dead straight.

He wipes his face blank, then draws in despair.

He knocks on the black, Victorian-style door with the golden lion knocker. The number 88 above it in gold, too.

Charles is on the other side of the door, on the other side of the studio that's not decked out like the hallway of that crazy glass and steel sci-fi apartment block the movie star lives in.

The red and gold carpet with the same pattern, the wall lights, even the oil painting of the old-time admiral on his warship in that elaborate gold frame.

No playing, it's all here, every detail recreated.

Going to these lengths? It is insane. And for true, I am impressed.

Charles opens the door.

Please, says Adonis. This time he's not reading the script.

I can't do this anymore. It was okay when we were on set, I could handle it. But now? It's killing me.

When I wake up in the morning, you're all I think about. When I'm on location, you're all I can think about. When I'm sleeping with other women, all I can see is your face.

He pauses. The desperation leaking out of this guy is unreal. Charles is just standing there, face blank, watching the performance.

I'm sick of tiptoeing around, says Adonis. I need to be with you. Forget that loser already, he's a shitty actor and an even shittier husband.

Please.

He stops. A sharp exhale, a roll of the head and shoulders, and he stands up straight again, face back to normal.

Wow, I say, clapping my hands. How do you do that?

Charles's face finally breaks. Much better, he says. What do you think, Sean?

All I can do is carry on clapping.

Charles says, Congratulations, looks like you've got the role.

Adonis grabs my hand and pumps it up and down, up and down.

Oh my god, he says, pumping up and down. Thank you, thank you so much.

When he finally stops trying to shake my arm out of its socket, he grabs his jacket and steps out.

I say, It's kind of nice making someone's day like that, no?

Indeed, says Charles.

Forty

This is me, in the dark, standing in front of Other Me's building again.

Because I went back to Charles's place after the auditions, looked to see if Other Me was in his room reading his book. But he wasn't.

So I'm waiting for him to come out again. Or return home.

Because let's face it: I'm frigging obsessed.

I brought my camera along so I can shoot some frames in case I'm here waiting for a while.

And so I can make this guy's portrait.

Because: I might be going crazy and imagining the whole thing?

I see two girls walking down the street towards me, dressed identically in stripy tops and matching trousers.

Just as I fire off a shot, a voice says, Oh hey, fancy seeing you here again.

I turn around, and Other Me is stood there. Standing tall, smiling warmly at me.

I advance the film and let the camera hang loose around my neck.

Oh hey, I say.

He says, I was just about to go and get something to eat. You hungry?

And I say, Sure, I could eat.

* * *

As the waitress walks past our table, Other Me says something to her in Mandarin. Not Mandarin like a foreigner, but Mandarin like my parents – the tone, the enunciation.

She stops, smiles at him and replies.

He laughs, says something else – and now they're in full-blown conversation.

I watch him as he talks. The arm slung across the back of the empty chair next to him, the way he casually touches her as he cracks a joke, the eyes laughing even though the mouth is only just about smiling.

I'm looking at a warped reflection of myself, and I can't stop watching.

The charisma, the easygoing vibe of the guy, it's everything I want.

Everything I don't have.

After she's gone, I say, You speak Chinese?

And he says, Why wouldn't I?

The canteen we're in fizzes and swells, Saturday night in Taipei getting on going.

The waitress is back at our table with a tray, and places on our table dish after dish of different meats, vegetables, seafood and sauces. In the middle between us is a gas stove, sunken into the surface, and on top of that, a large pot full of simmering broth.

Hot pot. I've only had this once with Charles, so I don't really know what I'm doing. I just stare at the array of ingredients in front of us.

Other Me? He takes his chopsticks, picks up a thin slice of red meat marbled with fat, dunks it into the broth four or five times, and puts it into his mouth, his eyes closed.

Oh man, he says. So good.

I do what he does, and he's not wrong.

What was your childhood like? I say.

Other Me, he doesn't bat an eyelid at the random line of questioning.

I grew up in Shropshire, he says. You know it?

I nod and I say, I grew up there too.

So you know what it was like, he says, fishing some vegetables out of the broth. Suburban. Kind of boring. Parents didn't really take much notice of me – apart from how I did at school. He chews. Yourself?

I watch him for a moment and I say, Pretty much the same.

And then I add: I kind of ignored the Taiwanese part of me, though.

He looks at me and he says, Yeah, I could tell. Why would you do that?

I think, Why wouldn't I?

And I watch him munch happily, belonging totally and utterly in the space he is in right now, and I think maybe I am completely losing my bananas.

Say cheese, I say.

FORTY-ONE

The crescent moon looks down at us, glowing through the car window. Adonis and me are in the front, Charles in the back. I hear a clicking sound.

Adonis is kneading his knuckles, cracking them one by one.

Charles leans forward in the space between us. He says, Don't be nervous. You were fantastic in the audition. Just let your training take over.

And I say, What he said.

Adonis nods and exhales three short sharp breaths, like he's about to get into a boxing ring or something. He hammers his head with his fists, says, LET'S DO THIS, and jumps out the car, slamming the door shut.

Charles makes this sort of snorting sound, exactly like the one Akemi does.

We watch him march to the front of the building, until he disappears through the big, glass, double doors.

I drive Charles's Audi round to the side of the building and park on a street studded with trees.

Charles moves into the passenger seat, gets out the tablet. He pokes the screen and hands it over to me.

In the living room, I see the movie star and his wife lounging around on the sofa, eating popcorn, watching a movie. One of his own, by the looks of things.

I hear a crunch. Charles is chomping on some popcorn. I watch him chew, and chew, and chew. And then chew and chew some more. It's around a minute I'm watching him eat, the crunching sound bouncing around inside the car, before he's finished chewing and finally swallows.

Would you like some? he says, offering me the pack.

* * *

Charles shakes my shoulder and I wake up with a start.

He points and says, You've got a bit of dribble there.

I wipe my mouth with my sleeve, look around. Trees, street lamps glowing orange in the dark, car interior.

Right.

Charles says, Look, there's our man.

On the tablet, I see Adonis at the door of the apartment, standing in the hallway. He's already in character – a tortured look on his face.

I say, What took him so long?

Perhaps he got lost, says Charles. Or maybe he had trouble with the fob.

Adonis knocks on the door, one-two-three.

On the tablet, I see the wife swinging her long legs off the movie star's lap. On a different camera feed, I see her reach the door, her back facing us.

She opens the door and says, Yes?

Please, says Adonis.

He's doing it just like he did in the audition, the anguished lover bearing his soul.

I look at Charles. He is mesmerized, face lit up by the tablet's blue-white glow. He's not munching popcorn anymore.

At this point, the wife, well she's freaking out. She's got no clue who this American hunk of a male is and what the hell he's doing there, saying he's in love with her etc.

The movie star, he pauses the film and walks over to investigate the ruckus.

He looks Adonis up and down, and he says, Who are you?

Adonis gives him the hard stare for a moment or two, and he says, I'm your wife's lover, that's who I am. All deep and growly.

Oh shit! This is even better than my new favourite soap opera. The movie star is quiet and the suspense is too much.

I compare Adonis and the movie star. Standing next to each other like that, Adonis has at least a two-head height advantage.

If I was a beautiful white woman like the movie star's wife here, I know who I would choose.

I'd throw myself into Adonis's big arms right there and then. Even if my husband wasn't abusing me.

The movie star, he finally turns to his wife and he says, Do you know this man?

No playing, this guy is ice cold.

The wife says, Of course I don't know him. I've never seen him in my life.

Right then, Adonis looks real hurt. He says, How could you say that in front of my face? After that night we shared together under the stars, devouring each other's naked bodies like two starved animals?

Oh ho, Charles says. He's improvising now.

For true, this is the best prank I have ever played on anyone in my life, ever.

FORTY-TWO

Window down, Charles lays his arm on the side of the car, steering with thumb and forefinger.

He says, Goodness, that was exhilarating. Wasn't that exhilarating?

I say, Super exhilarating. Our man smashed it in there, no?

Charles says, Smashed it indeed. He says, I couldn't have pulled this off without you. What a fantastic idea.

Splish, splash, splosh.

This thing we've done, are doing right now, it's fun. Me and Charles, sharing a moment, and it's like I'm finally bonding with someone the way I should have bonded with my dad.

I think about Other Me and how he just seems to belong. And in Charles's car, after the adrenaline and the craziness of the prank we just pulled, I'm thinking maybe I'm starting to feel like that too.

Like this is the place for me.

I'm not gonna lie, I say. I thought the guy would have reacted a bit more—

Crazy?

Right.

(After Adonis got the door shut in his face, they just brushed their teeth and went to bed like normal. Backs to each other.)

Charles sticks his hand out the window, fingers spread out. He's enjoying the feeling of the air against his skin.

He says, We've had a bigger impact on them than it seems. Trust me.

I watch Charles drive for a minute. The breeze plays with his white hair. He has the tiniest of smiles on his face.

Happy, shiny eyes. Less giddy, like he was at the bowling alley, more content.

No, satisfied.

He pushes a cassette into the car stereo, more of that dreamy French piano music.

I open my own window, get some of that cool night breeze. Outside, as the car moves slow with the traffic, bright neon flashes and blurs, up, up, up into the sky. Streets still thick.

I say, Debussy, right?

Right, Charles says. *Doctor Gradus ad Parnassum.*

He turns to me, points his finger at me. Played by Chia Chen though.

He says, Taiwanese pianists, you see, they have more discipline, more focus, more technique. You can hear it in the recordings, if you listen closely enough.

This guy's fingers must be moving at insane speeds up and down those piano keys. The image in my head: those fingers dancing around, little wisps of smoke starting up until the keys catch fire. The way this guy is playing, you'd think only a machine was capable of that.

I think about how my parents made me do extra study time after school and at weekends for hours and hours, hours and hours. When all I wanted to do was draw Superman and Flash comics.

I bet this Chia Chen didn't even know who Superman was as a kid. I bet his entire world was eighty-eight black and white keys.

I did get As though. You never saw my parents' eyes light up the way they did when there were As all round. *Ding ding ding.*

And that feeling when their smiles spread and words of pride came out of their mouths (mostly to their friends), and they were beaming and I was getting blasted (indirectly) by those rays ...

Fuzzy.

I say to Charles, You could say the same about Chinese pianists, too, I suppose.

I don't know what I've just said though, because Charles's face turns.

He says, They are nowhere near the same.

But when you think about it, we're pretty much Chinese, right?

I don't know what I've just said, because Charles's face has gone atomic.

He turns to me and he says, My family has been in Taiwan for centuries. Akemi and me, we have aborigine blood flowing in our veins.

He says, China? China is a power-mad maniac obsessed with control. It uses its might to lean on nations and organizations. It will do anything to ensure that our independence is not acknowledged.

It insists we are one of its states, he scoffs.

Chinese Taipei? he says. Disgusting.

This is just about as worked up as I've seen Charles get. Except for when he first told me about his dad's boss.

He says, Have you heard of the 228 incident?

I shake my head.

Of course you haven't. He shakes his head, blows out a sigh. Did your parents teach you nothing?

I say, Not really, no.

He says, I suggest you look it up.

I tell him I'll do that.

And I look out at that pretty neon again, and the piano music washes over me and out the window.

Forty-Three

Akemi's mouth makes the shape of an O when she does the thing. She's swaying and she's got her head tilted back and her eyes are closed and yeah, she is for sure feeling it.

I watch her performing this song that she wrote on the piano – kind of Lauryn Hill, kind of The xx – and I think how funny it is that this is exactly the same pained–ecstatic look she had on just a bit ago when we were having sex on the sofa I'm on right now: me struggling to get my trousers and socks off, so I just sack the socks off completely, sitting down so she can ease herself onto my cock while I also minimize the chance of being exposed as less than adequate in bed (I bet you a million pounds Other Me doesn't have this problem), and as we settle into an irregular rhythm, her ragged breath in my ear, the sexual frenzy descends, I start losing myself – but not before I marvel at the fact I haven't prematurely

169

ejaculated or lost my erection – so much so that I think I might say something I don't actually mean, because let's face it, this girl has been the closest thing I've had to real intimacy, this girl whose body is taut and angular and warm, and she knows, somehow she knows, so she claps her hand over my mouth as the fucking turns desperate, eye contact that messes me up something crazy, her teeth on my lips and that's it, I'm done, and she's done, and we crumple onto the sofa, just lying there while we listen to the blood in our ears.

After a couple minutes, I ask her whether we should really be fucking in her father's house, on her father's sofa. Whether we should maybe go to her place in future.

On account of it being, you know, disrespectful.

She turns to me and scoffs. Since she refused to be what he wanted her to be, she tells me, her dad doesn't care what she does.

The last chord from the piano floats out into the corners of the penthouse's living room, before disappearing into nothingness.

I say, I didn't know you were a musician. I thought you just worked at the reception in the hotel and that was it.

She swivels around to face me and says, Not everyone walks around flaunting their talent around their neck.

Well, you're really good, I say. Like, record deal, playing-in-front-of-big-audiences good.

She laughs and she says, I guess that's the plan. A bit crazy when you think about it.

I think about my own photographic fantasies – cover shoots, gallery shows – and I say, No. There's nothing silly about that at all.

She says, It's amazing how differently you see your dreams when people around you take them seriously.

Charles doesn't approve? I ask.

She tells me about how her father would rather she went into medicine, or law. Something prestigious, yet lucrative. Or if she was adamant about the music thing, the least she could do was become a performer of classical music, not this pop malarkey.

She's nearly done saving up to move to Tokyo, she tells me. The music scene there is better than it is in Taipei. And, more importantly, her mother is out there.

A few more weeks, and she's on a plane out of here.

The information slaps me in the face. A few more weeks? What am I going to do when she's gone?

Because, let's face it, I like this girl.

I half-think about telling her she should stay, but instead I ask her why she doesn't just ask Charles for the money, seeing as he clearly has enough to spare. Easy.

And she tells me she doesn't want to take money from him, or anything else for that matter, because a) he treated her mother like shit, b) she wants to prove to him that she can make it on her own without his money, and c) she wants to be able to support her mum with her own money eventually.

I think about my own mum, and how she would guilt trip me for moving away to London, telling me how loyal and good her friends' sons were because they stayed at home to look after their parents.

I ask Akemi what happened between Charles and her mother.

She tells me her mother needed to move back to Japan when she was little, because her father, Akemi's grandfather, was in bad health. He needed looking after, and even though she begged and pleaded, begged and pleaded, Charles refused to move with her.

Because he was never going to leave Taiwan. His life was here, and if that's what she wanted to do, fine, he wasn't going to stop her.

So she left.

Akemi says, That was around seven years ago. And because my dad was the one who could provide for me better, I stayed with him. Even though I desperately wanted to be with my mother.

We visited her every school holiday, she says. Or she would come here.

Then she adds: But it's not the same really.

We sit in silence for a bit, and the meaning of our conversation balloons.

* * *

Do you know that saying, every man has his double? I ask Akemi, as we sit at the breakfast bar in Charles's kitchen, munching on some strawberries.

I think I've heard it somewhere before, she says.

I ask, What do you make of it?

She says, I read once that the universe is infinite. And if the universe is infinite, then there's infinite possibilities that there are planets like ours out there – planets that developed exactly like ours, with people on them exactly like us, but with the tiniest differences.

She picks up a strawberry from the dish, plump and red, and takes a bite. Like, maybe that little scar you have in the corner of your left eye, maybe there's a Sean in another galaxy that has that scar in the corner of his right eye. And maybe there's an Akemi somewhere in space, that plays the guitar instead of the piano, and stayed with her mother instead of her father.

Interesting, I say. But what about on this planet. Do you think we all have a double on Earth?

There are around seven billion people in the world,

right? she says. I suppose the chances of one of those people looking like you, or me, are pretty good.

Yeah, I say, but looking *exactly* like us? With another Sean that has that scar in *exactly* the same spot? And the *exact* same tattoo?

She looks at me, bemused. Why are you asking me all this?

And I say, Oh, no reason.

FORTY-FOUR

I watch a picture of myself appear like magic, warping and wobbling under chemical ripples as I swirl it around with tongs.

Except it's not really a picture of me, but a picture of Other Me – a portrait I made of him when we had hot pot in the canteen the other night.

And this, this is straight-up proof that I am not imagining this guy, or going crazy.

I hang the picture to dry on the line, flip on the lights.

It's not a candid picture, I asked him if I could make his portrait. And unlike me, he didn't arch his eyebrows to make his eyes look bigger – which has the effect of making me look surprised all the time – or throw out a cheesy grin to avoid the probability of looking awkward in a photo.

In this picture, he's just staring straight into the lens. Eyes smiling. A slight upturn at the corners of his mouth.

No lie, I am still creeped the hell out.

But on the flip side, this guy, this other me, he's like ...

A better me.

In every way.

The perfect me.

Like I'm the prototype, he's the polished, finished version.

The whole thing is bizarre, fucked-up, fascinating. But where does that leave me?

I think about Mia, and I think about Tanner, and I think that maybe if I was more like Other Me, then I'd still be in London, still with Mia.

And we'd be happy. Or happier than we were.

And Tanner would be an insignificant stroke of slug slime that would never have streaked its way across our path.

Probably.

I think that maybe I would not have to be a surly douchebag everywhere I go.

Seriously though. What kind of name is Tanner?

Portrait now dry, I unpeg it and look down at the image in my hands, this off-kilter version of me that seems to have the answer to the question I'm asking.

I pour the chemicals in the tray away, flip the lights off, and walk out the darkroom.

FORTY-FIVE

We're in a barbecue joint, neon signs for American beer companies buzzing next to my head, my arse squeaking on the cushy, deep-red leather of the booth.

Other Me, he has a forkful of burnt ends, closes his eyes, chews and says, Oh boy. This, this is just ridiculous. Here, you've got to try some of this.

Before I can decline, he spears another chunk of meat and holds it in front of my mouth, and the intimacy is so shocking that all I can do is open up like a baby and let the choo-choo train in.

The meat is juicy, and tender, and good, but right now I find myself wanting the small and varied flavour bombs that you get from dim sum. The soy sauce, the spring onion, the ginger, the garlic, the vinegar, the rice wine.

Umami for days.

Wait, you've got a little sauce there, he says, and he

leans forward to wipe the corner of my mouth with his napkin.

So, am I right? he says, eyes on mine, waiting for me to break down the meat enough so I can swallow, and for the surely enthusiastic response.

No playing, you are right, I say.

Over the course of the evening, we've shot the breeze. We've talked about growing up, photography, this crazy, ugly beautiful city that is an all-out assault on the senses.

I sip my microbrewery bottled beer and I say, Have you heard of the 228 incident?

He puts his knife and fork down, nods while he chews. Of course I have, he says.

What's that all about then?

Well, it's pretty long and complicated, he says. But in a nutshell?

In a nutshell.

He pulls on his beer and signals to the waiter for another one.

So, it's the end of World War Two. Japan surrenders to the Allies, and Taiwan is now in the hands of the Republic of China after fifty years of Japanese rule.

He says, But the Taiwanese people? They're pissed, on account of the Kuomintang – the new ruling government – taking their property for no reason, stopping people from getting involved in politics. The Kuomintang are bad with money, so there's mad inflation, unemployment, food shortages, a huge black market. Corrupt shit.

One day, it's 27 February 1947, state Tobacco Monopoly Bureau agents beat on a forty-year-old widow because they think she's selling contraband cigarettes. The Bureau, it deals with tobacco, booze, tea, stuff like that, so pushing non-state-sanctioned product is very non-cool for them. The people who see this on the street, they're mad because, well, wouldn't you be if you saw government officials giving a defenceless person a beat down?

The waiter comes back and deposits another bottle of beer on our table. Other Me, he doffs an imaginary cap and he says, *Gracias*.

So the next day, he says, on the twenty-eighth, you've got people rising up in front of the Bureau building, raging at the way they treated this widow, raging at the way they're being treated themselves. And then a bunch of soldiers roll in and start shooting.

News of the rebellion gets out and the whole island gets in on the action. At this point, the governor, Chen Yi, he starts freaking out, calls in more military backup. And before you know it, the National Revolutionary Army is everywhere, murdering people left, right and centre. Around 28,000 people die in the massacre.

Twenty-eighth of February, I say. That's why it's called the 228 incident.

Bingo, says Other Me.

I say, Then what?

Other Me has another mouthful of food, wipes his mouth with a napkin. In a nutshell?

In a nutshell.

Thirty-eight years of martial law, which people here refer to as the White Terror. In the beginning, you've got troops killing and looting and raping. Bodies all over the streets. And then as the years go on, you speak out against the government, you go to prison. Sometimes you get executed. It's 1987 before Taiwan starts making moves towards democracy and a pro-independence movement.

I sit there for a minute, digest the information as I digest the burnt ends.

Other Me, he goes back to eating.

He says, I can't believe you don't know any of this. It was worse than Tiananmen Square.

I think about my parents – too busy and too distant to talk to me about these things.

I think about the white town I grew up in, my white friends, the singular British bubble I have existed in.

And then I wipe it all from my mind and I say, Ah well. Want another beer?

Forty-Six

Ni shi na guo ren? says the robot woman in my ears.

Wo shi Taiwan ren, I say back to her.

Ni shi na guo ren? repeats the robot woman in my ears.

Wo shi Yingguo ren, I say back to her.

Charles appears on the roof terrace and sits down next to me.

His mouth moves but I don't hear anything. I take out my earbuds and I say, Excuse me?

He says, Learning Mandarin?

I pause my audio teacher and put my phone down. I guess I thought I should, I say. I've been here long enough.

He looks at me, an approving look, and it makes me feel like I'm doing something worthwhile.

He stands up again, puts his hand on my shoulder, and he says, I'm impressed.

He says, I would think the first phrase you said was the correct one, though.

He pauses for a bit, and then goes back inside.

I turn around, watch him until he disappears from view.

I put my earbuds back in, un-pause my audio robot teacher.

Ni shi na guo ren? she asks.

Wo shi Taiwan ren, I say back to her.

* * *

I am parched, because that's what two hours of speaking rudimentary Mandarin phrases will do to you.

When I go inside to get some water, Charles is sat at the breakfast bar, reading a magazine with a cup of tea. The look on his face – tickled.

I grab some water from the fridge full of precision-stacked bottles and sit down opposite him.

I say, What's funny?

He spins the magazine round so I can see. It's a celeb rag, like the one the auntie in the laundrette was reading.

I lean in, and I recognize the picture of the people on the page, on account of it being the movie star and his wife. The text is all in Chinese though, so I ask Charles what the article says.

He says, Remember in the car when you said you thought our little prank would have had more of an impact?

I feel the icy water trickle down my throat and into my belly, blooming.

Well, he says, tapping the magazine, this says that they're breaking up. Due to the wife's cheating ways, of course.

And the kid? I say.

The son goes with the mother, says Charles, shaking his head, a man whose fortune is getting better and better by the minute. He's got a far-off look in his eyes, satisfaction curling his mouth upwards.

I say, What are you thinking about?

His eyes focus on mine, and he says, I'm imagining the face on the movie star's father, covered in egg. His precious boy – cuckolded and divorced. No wife, no child. The shame, it must be unbearable.

Job done then, I say. We smashed it right?

Charles closes the magazine, pushes it to the side and picks up his teacup.

Not yet, he says.

FORTY-SEVEN

The walls are white and, for the most part, blank. There's no furniture, except for a brown leather sofa, smack bang in the middle of the room, almost camouflaging itself into the wooden floorboards.

It's a small space, but with the lack of stuff inside, it looks cavernous.

There's no television. No audio system. No bookcase. No plants. No lamps. No shelves on the wall.

Nothing.

Apart from the wall facing the sofa. Hung up there, is a giant print of a photograph.

The photograph – it's a night photograph.

This photograph, it's got the Taipei 101 in it – with long-exposure light trails swooping their way across it.

This photograph, it must be three-by-three metres or something – the size of canvases you see in art galleries.

You live here? I say.

Yep, Other Me says. Nice, huh?

He says, Have a seat. Want a drink? Maybe some tea?

I sit down on the sofa, and now I have nowhere else to look except this horrific, gigantic print in front of me.

I say, Sure, I'll have some tea.

He comes back with a teapot covered by a knitted tea cosy with multicoloured bobbles on it, two fine bone-china teacups with saucers, and a stripy blue and white jar.

I watch as he deftly pours the tea, lifting the pot higher as the pour goes on.

He hands me one of the cups on its saucer, and he says, Biscuit?

I say, Sure, I'll have a biscuit.

He takes the lid off the jar and offers it to me – inside it's full of custard creams.

I take one, and I see that he's lifting his cup in cheers, so I do the same before taking a sip.

The tea takes me by surprise, because it's English breakfast tea, the kind I would drink buckets of back home – tea I haven't drunk since I've been here.

It hits a spot somewhere deep down in me, and for a second I miss home.

Other Me gets up off his knees and sits down on the sofa next to me. It's big enough for three, maybe even four, but regardless, he plonks himself right next to me, his thigh pressed on mine once he's settled.

I try and figure out where to put my cup and saucer – the arm of the sofa? My lap? – and decide on the floor, underneath the sofa so I don't accidentally kick it over and spill it.

What the hell is that? I say, nodding at the light-trail print.

You like it? he says.

I fucking hate it, I say. It offends every fibre of my being, I say.

Whoa, he says. Easy tiger, I took that myself.

What?

He slouches further into the sofa, hands in his pockets, admiring his work. His elbow digs into my hip.

Yep, he says. On a digital camera, too.

What?

Is this guy serious? This is all too much.

I like the ease of it, he says, running his hand through his perfectly combed hair.

I can't believe what I am hearing, these blasphemous words coming out of what appears to be my mouth, so I decide to just shut up for a bit.

* * *

Who's the dude you're living with then? says Other Me, as he pours more tea into our cups.

This takes me by surprise, because I haven't mentioned Charles to him before. He doesn't even know where I live. At least, I think he doesn't know where I live.

I say, What do you mean?

Other Me, he says, You know, the dapper, white-haired gentleman I see you hanging out with on that roof terrace over there. He nods in the direction of Charles's place, which, of course, is opposite this flat we're sitting in right now.

He laughs and he says, You're not the only one with a telephoto lens, homie.

I curse my ignorance and my arrogance, and I say, He's called Charles. I'm working for him, and in return, I get to stay at his place.

For real? says Other Me.

For real, I say.

Must be nice, says Other Me. Living large in that penthouse.

Yeah, I suppose it is, I say, thinking about the luxury of Charles's place, the sheer space of it, and how already I'm taking it for granted, forgetting I used to share a poky one-bedroom flat in Hackney just a couple months ago.

He says, What kind of work are you doing for him?

I say, Just photographing interiors, nothing exciting.

Huh, interesting, says Other Me, and he's quiet for a moment, blowing on his tea to cool it down.

He looks back at me, eyes smiling slightly.

What about that girl I've seen you with? he says.

That's Akemi, I say. She's Charles's daughter.

Other Me makes an *I see* kind of face. He says, She's pretty, no? In an unconventional way, I mean.

And I say, Yeah, I suppose she is.

FORTY-EIGHT

The projector flickers white light onto the wall as the small screening room emerges, slow and smooth, from the darkness.

Me, Akemi and Charles, we're all sitting in a row of reclining chairs, me in the middle.

Watching the end credits rise, backed by an orchestra of swoon-inducing strings.

Akemi nudges me with her elbow. That was fun, watching that film for the fiftieth time.

Charles nudges me with his elbow. He says, He got a Golden Horse award for that performance. Unbelievable.

He beckons me to lean over, and he whispers in my ear, We've taken his wife, we've taken his child.

He whispers, And you're absolutely right, we should take his career next.

I'm thinking, What? I never suggested that we take his career.

Or did I?

Akemi says to me softly, Why can't we watch something different for once? Like some vintage Masahiro Shinoda or something?

I look at Charles, and he's being serious.

And I whisper back to him, I didn't suggest we take his career?

Charles frowns at me. He says, Are you pulling my leg? We had a conversation about it the other night. A couple of days ago. Outside the building. Remember?

I flip through the index cards of my brain, try and remember where I was two nights ago, because I for sure don't remember having this conversation that Charles is adamant we had.

What are you two talking about? says Akemi.

Before we can answer, she gets out her phone and chuckles at a message she's received.

She leans over and shows me, the screen lighting her face with a ghostly glow.

I look at the screen, and what I'm looking at is a selfie. Of me. Pulling a comedy face, tongue sticking out, eyes crossed.

I didn't take that selfie, and no playing, I didn't send it to Akemi.

Or did I?

You're such a joker, she says.

Charles says, I think your mind is going soft, son. Perhaps you should start playing Go with me.

The padded walls close in, and I feel like I am going to be crushed.

FORTY-NINE

I knock on the door, one-two-three.

I listen, but there is no movement, no sound on the other side.

I knock again, louder this time, the edge of my fist turning it into a thump.

Behind it, I hear soft footsteps approaching.

The door opens, and Other Me is standing there.

Oh hey, he says. Want to come in?

I walk past him into the living room, stand by the sofa like a lemon.

He says, Want to sit down?

So I sit on the sofa.

He says, Want a drink?

And I say, No, thanks.

He sits down next to me and he says, So, what's good?

For true, the charm just oozes out of him.

I look at him for a second. The crossed legs, the arms extending to the top corners of the sofa, the body pointed in the direction of mine.

Crisp white T-shirt, loose black trousers, white socks and black slides. His hair is damp and combed, and I smell the earthy body wash he used in the shower.

I hear the cars driving past slow on the street below, punctuated by the frequent zip of scooters. Someone somewhere is playing an old-sounding Taiwanese pop song on the radio, and the shrill female voice wobbles its pentatonic notes in through the open window and into the room.

I say, Have you been talking to Charles and Akemi?

Nuh-uh, he says, picking some fluff off his trousers.

Although, he says, a little side-smile creeping up, I wouldn't mind getting to know Akemi a bit more intimately, if you know what I mean.

Of course I know what he means, he's just confirmed what I've known ever since I clapped eyes on him through my viewfinder. And here he is, right in front of me: the perfect guy who shagged Akemi better than I could.

And I am jealous, and afraid. The polished version of me, Sean 2.0, already making moves.

This is *my* life, I say.

It sure is, he says.

FIFTY

I pick up my camera from the bedside table.

I lie down on my bed and play with the focus ring to help me calm down.

I left Other Me's flat in a weird way – like, I'd made my point, told him to not get involved in my shit anymore.

But at the same time, he didn't really say he would stop.

He just smiled at me in the way that he does. Made agreeable noises.

Offered me a biscuit.

When I got up to leave, he told me he'd see me later. Patted me on the back.

And now I am fully spooked, because what if he's lying and he has been talking to Charles and Akemi?

What if he muscles in on the thing me and Akemi have got going on?

What if he's talking to Charles, giving him great ideas, making himself more valuable to Charles than I am?

There is no way Akemi and Charles wouldn't realize that there are two of us, identical in looks but completely different in behaviour.

No way.

That one of us is more competent, more funny, more handsome, more charming, more clever and more rewarding to be around.

Let's face it, Akemi would never look at me the same again. She would never forgive me. For lying to her, for pretending to be someone else, for tricking her into having sex with me.

I can see now – the whole thing with Akemi was a terrible idea. And I'm not altogether sure I can take that kind of rejection.

Again.

And because Sean 2.0 is better than me in every way, that leaves me . . .

Nowhere.

With nothing.

No home. No money. Alone in not one, but two countries.

Sometimes, two of something is really not better than one.

I get off the bed, walk to the window and look

out – barely perceptible clouds in the night sky drifting above the blanket of lights in the city below.

I fire off a quick shot of the scene, the light in my room just bright enough so my reflection makes it more of a yellow-tinted self-portrait than a landscape.

Out there, probably in that building, is Other Me.

Out there, he's probably thinking about how he can take me out of the equation, get in on this good, but fragile thing I've somehow managed to build for myself.

I mean, why wouldn't he?

In here, I'm thinking, Fuck that.

I remember Charles saying something to me one time.

Victorious warriors win first, and then they go to war.

I sling my camera round my neck, and head off outside.

FIFTY-ONE

I knock on the door, one—

It swings open inward, and Other Me is already walking down the hallway to the living room.

He says, Hey man, come in.

I close the door behind me, and follow him.

In the living room, he is sitting on the sofa, quiet and calm, like he's waiting for something inevitable.

He says, I didn't expect to see you again so soon. What a pleasure.

I sit down next to him, facing him, and I say, To be honest, I didn't either.

I decide to just come out with it.

Who the fuck are you?

He looks at me and laughs.

You know who I am, Sean.

The answer makes no sense, offers zero clarity.

I say, You look like me, but you are not me. We are completely different.

He leans forward, so close to me his nose touches mine.

He says, Only at this moment in time, homie.

He reaches into his pocket, takes out his phone. Starts dialling a number.

What are you doing? I say.

Mia? he says, looking right at me, smiling. Hi.

And then, I lose it. Because interfering with Akemi and Charles is one thing. But butting into Mia's life? That's a goddamn step too far.

I grab the phone, end the call and toss it away, and before he can react, before he can say anything, I'm on him, smashing my fist onto his face, over and over, I'm someone I don't recognize, taken over by a rage, and Other Me, he doesn't do anything, all he does is take it, a smile on his face as I pummel away, even when the blood starts to flow from his nose and his lips and his cut eye, even when the effort draws sweat from my brow, drip-drip-dripping, and his smile turns into a laugh, not a chuckle, not a cackle, but a deep laugh of contentment – this laugh, it tugs at something deep inside me, so raw I take my camera from my neck and bring it straight down onto his cheek, no playing, it feels like I've been at it for days, I'm tired, my arm is numb, and I stop to catch my breath.

I retreat to the other end of the sofa.

I look at him, his face now swollen, and red.

And in this perfect face gone ugly – my face – I see it all.

I see the split, the two sides of me, one side overpowered by the other until it has all but disappeared.

I see what that disappearance has done to me.

I see that I am a half-person.

I get up, start to leave, and he says, Hey, where you going? We're not done yet.

Stay away from me, I say. Stay away from Charles and Akemi. Stay away from Mia.

And as I walk away, his laughter follows until I'm out of the flat and the door has closed shut behind me.

FIFTY-TWO

For some reason, the goddamn door won't open. The key won't go into the keyhole.

I hold the little piece of metal up to my face, looking to see if maybe it's changed shape or something, suddenly grown too wide to fit into its slot. I can't really see it all that well though, on account of my shaking hand.

I grab my wrist with my other hand, will the key to go in and turn, and finally I am back in the safety of the penthouse.

* * *

After I've stumbled to the fridge, got me some water, chugged the whole lot down and sat down at the table, the kitchen is quiet.

The long pendant light illuminates the table. But around me, everything is dark.

I look at my camera on the table, the edge of its smooth, matt, chrome metal body blotched with dried blood.

His blood.

My blood.

* * *

My body feels like it's vibrating at hyper-speeds.

Effectively, I have just beat the shit out of myself, and I don't think I will ever be able to shake the terrible image of my own fucked-up face, for as long as I live.

To calm myself down I choose a bottle of Japanese single malt whisky from Charles's collection, pour myself a glass, down it.

I feel the flush instantly, the pressure in my face, my heart beating even faster than it was before.

Bad idea, Sean.

* * *

Half an hour later, after some panicked deep breathing, I think I am maybe calming down.

I think about Other Me, and I understand now. I understand why he was so different to me.

201

Why he seemed to occupy the space he occupied so fully.

Why he was so . . . comfortable. Wherever he was, whoever he was with.

FIFTY-THREE

Charles Hu emerges from the darkness, a reassuring sight in pyjamas if ever I saw one.

He sits down opposite me, eyeing up the paraphernalia spread out in front of me with an intrigued look.

Still, he doesn't say anything, except, I'm having trouble sleeping.

I pour whisky into the glass and offer it to him.

He takes a sip and he says, Your idea to ruin the movie star's career – it's been running through my head all night. The different possibilities, how it could all play out, how doing so would devastate him and, more importantly, his father – utterly.

He pats me on the shoulder and he says, I know I keep saying it, but I really think it's fate that we ended up together. None of this would have been possible without you.

He says, For the first time in a long time, I feel like myself. And for that, he says, I thank you.

Under the glow of the pendant light, in the strange small hours of the night, Charles seems to have softened.

He reminds me of my dad, in the days before he got really bad, before he had to go to the hospital.

You're welcome, I say.

I say, I should thank you, too. You and Akemi.

For what? he says.

I say, For helping me out when I was in a bad spot.

I say, For making me feel like I'm supposed to be here.

He passes me the glass.

The pleasure is all ours, he says. Truly.

FIFTY-FOUR

A plinky-plonk version of 'Looking with My Eyes' plays on the speakers.

Zit Boy brings over a platter of eight doughnuts, places it on the table in front of me.

I look at the doughy blobs, glistening with sugar and fat under the white gleam of the strip light.

The thought of putting one in my mouth makes me feel kind of sick, and I think that maybe this time, me and Charles should have gone to a decent tea house.

But Charles, for some reason, he loves these doughnuts.

Speaking of Charles, where is he?

He is fifteen minutes late, and the man makes it a point to never be late, to never not follow the right etiquette for any given situation.

I get out my phone and call him, but it rings to answer machine.

I look out the window, I pick up a doughnut, and I munch.

* * *

I am back at the penthouse, on account of Charles still not showing up at Monsieur Donut after half an hour.

I check the living room.

I check the kitchen.

I check the roof terrace.

Nothing.

I check the bedrooms.

I check the bathrooms.

I check the screening room.

Nothing.

Back in the living room, I call out, Charles!

I wait, and I listen, and there is no answer.

Just silence.

For true, something is very not right.

I flop onto the sofa.

On the coffee table in front of me, I see Charles's tablet.

I pick it up, check the hidden-camera feeds in the movie star's apartment.

And standing right there, in the corner of the movie star's bedroom, is Charles.

Dead straight. Dead still. Staring straight ahead at the blank wall an inch from his face.

FIFTY-FIVE

On the street, I look up, and the double-helix tower looms.

Like before, I go around the building, open the gates to the underground garage and slip in.

I walk past the Range Rovers and the Aston Martins and the Jaguars.

Inside the lobby, it's quiet. I walk up to the security desk, where Benny the guard is busy playing *Mario* on his Game Boy. I hear the descending electronic bleep as the plumber jumps down into a warp pipe.

Hey, I say to Benny.

Uh-huh, says Benny.

* * *

The lift *dings*, floor 88.

I step out into the corridor. The red carpet with the

golden floral pattern, the window at the end. It's like I was here only yesterday.

I walk towards the window. The corridor is a vacuum.

I stomp on the ground, there is no sound.

I hum, and even though I can feel my vocal cords vibrating, nothing comes out of my mouth.

The window stretches away then nears, stretches away then nears.

I look left, I look right. The proportions of the corridor, they're all wrong, irregular angles, shifting.

I look back at the window, and I see a figure there with its back to me, staring away from me.

Hey! I say, soundlessly.

The figure half-turns its head to look in my direction, a painted face revealed, then it moves left and out of sight.

I walk past the oil painting of the old-time admiral on his warship, his gaze smug and superior. It looks bigger than it did the last time, looming.

I turn the corner, and the figure is nowhere to be seen.

Here it is. Apartment 88, with its heavy, black Victorian door and golden lion knocker.

I take the key out of my pocket.

I insert it into the keyhole, and I turn.

* * *

Inside the apartment, it's dark.

The air is moist, hot, suffocating. It presses on me.

I flip the light switch on the wall, but nothing happens.

Weird. I try the switch a few more times, but the lights refuse to come on.

I click my torch on, and head to the master bedroom.

* * *

In here, the air is even closer.

In the darkness, the room feels small.

Like a broom cupboard.

But the beam of light from my torch sweeps this way and that, and my eyes tell me it's the same size as it was before.

Cavernous.

In the movie star's bedroom, I find Charles in the corner, standing with his back to me.

Dead straight. Dead still.

Staring straight ahead at the wall.

Charles, I hiss. What the hell are you doing?

I shine the light on his face, and his eyes are focused on something way beyond the wall.

His lips are moving, barely whispered words coming out of his mouth.

What is that, Hokkien?

I look closer, and he is shivering in the heat.

Charles, I hiss. We need to get out of here, before the movie star busts us.

Right behind me, I hear a voice say, *Guo lai?*

Seductive and singing and sly.

Charles! I hiss, shaking his shoulder.

He turns to look at me.

What are you doing here? he says, calmly, looking back at the wall.

What the fuck are *you* doing here? I say.

This is super not part of the plan.

You can't see him? says Charles.

I look at the wall he's staring at, and I say, Who?

My father, says Charles, smiling. He's right there.

Come, he says, grabbing my arm, his grip causing the muscles it touches to ring with pain.

I hear a shuffling sound behind me, and I am afraid, and I think, Fuck this.

But before I can pull my arm free, he lifts his foot, moves it forward, and I watch as it sinks into the wall.

FIFTY-SIX

Picture a young Charles Hu, fifteen years old.

He is on his knees, surrounded by his mother and his seven brothers and sisters.

And his daddy, he's lying on his back, raised up in front of them.

Naaamooooo aaaaaaaamiiiiiituoooofooooooo . . .

Naaamooooo aaaaaaaamiiiiiituoooofooooooo . . .

Naaamooooo aaaaaaaamiiiiiituoooofooooooo . . .

The monk drone, it goes on and on.

The smoke from the joss sticks, it snakes and it swirls.

But young Charles, he can't chant anymore. His throat is dry, and his voice is failing.

Because unlike his brothers and sisters, he's been chanting for three days straight.

Because if he doesn't, his daddy's spirit won't be protected on its way to rebirth.

He doesn't eat. He doesn't sleep. He barely drinks.

For three days, he has been steadfast. No tears, by his daddy's side.

But now, something changes.

A high-pitched wail, it comes out of young Charles, long, and slow, and ragged.

And young Charles, he collapses.

His brothers and sisters, they try to pick him up, his body convulsing in their arms as he sobs and screams silently.

They try to pick him up, but he is dead weight.

They try to pick him up, but he is broken.

FIFTY-SEVEN

What do you think you are doing? says Charles.

He's snapped out of whatever weird state he was in.

The lights have come on, and the sudden brightness stabs at my eyes.

We're on the floor, on account of me tackling Charles to the ground to shake him out of his crazy.

Um, trying to get us out of here before the movie star comes back and we go to jail? I say.

I don't want to go to jail, I say.

You're welcome, I say.

Charles, he gets to his feet and looks into the corner of the room he was just standing in, despair colouring his face.

No, he says, no no no no no.

The despair turns to rage.

He points his finger at me and he says, You westerners. Always thinking about yourselves.

He shouts, Do you want to know why I take you to those nauseating doughnut cafes and bowling alleys?

He screams, Because I like to remind myself of how vacuous you westerners are. Self-centred. Obsessed with nothing but your own pleasure, your own petty wants.

I look at this man, shrunken and stiff, like he's riddled with chronic arthritis.

The bitterness bristling from his twisted face.

And as flecks of spit detonate from his mouth and his finger jabs the air in front of my face, I think about how wrong I've got it all – how I've been a junkie for this man's false praise.

I think of all the people I've allowed to be my compass.

I think about who I am. Who I really am.

FIFTY-EIGHT

The early-autumn sun throws dappled light that dances. Leaves from the great tree I'm sitting under touching the ground gently around me.

The air is crisp, the air is cold. It's 5 pm, and Kensington's workers stride with purpose, heading for the Tube on their way home.

I keep my eyes locked on the gallery's entrance, the steps leading up to it, and it feels like she's never going to appear.

But sure enough, after a few minutes, there she is.

The sight of Mia after so long, it shocks me, and I am so overwhelmed that I feel that feeling before you start crying.

That ache in the throat.

I watch her walk down the steps, the heels of her boots

tapping, the burnt orange of her beret matching perfectly the colour of the trees.

I stand up when she nears.

Hey, I say.

She smiles at me, and she says, Hey.

* * *

Golden hour light floods the room, the kind of light photographers' wet dreams are made of.

The warm breeze pats the long, white curtains, and through the window I can see trees swaying, branches full of bright, green leaves.

I hear the soft sound of faraway kids playing their faraway games.

Under that, a lawnmower drones its way along a lawn somewhere.

We're in bed. Mia, she's facing me, tracing my lip with her finger.

I look at the brown of her eyes, the way her hair falls delicately across her face and shoulders.

She smiles, turns around so she's got her back to me. I feel the warmth of her naked body on mine.

She's got her hair tied up in a bun, the soft skin of her neck exposed.

I place my lips on the base of her neck.

I feel the fuzz stick to my lips as my warm, damp breath bounces off her skin.

I breathe in deep the smell of her coconut shampoo, and I fall asleep.

Fifty-Nine

I wake up, alone.

Out the window, I see skyscrapers and power lines and tower blocks.

I turn onto my other side, and I see the immaculately curated furnishings of my room in Charles's penthouse.

And I remember what happened last night.

How me and Charles got into some crazy shit at the movie star's apartment.

How I left him to his warped obsession.

I get up, go to the en-suite bathroom, and piss a piss of eternity.

* * *

When I walk into the kitchen, Akemi is sitting at the breakfast bar, staring into space.

Oh hey, I say. Can I make you a cup of tea?

The way she's looking at me, I know for sure something is not right. She looks like she did when we first met, that Antarctic chill blowing.

She says, I spoke to my dad.

I fill the kettle with water, put it on to boil.

She says, He told me what you two have been up to. Sneaking around, messing with that actor and his family.

I have no defences to line up, so I say nothing.

I put a teabag into a cup, pour in the boiling water and feel the steam cling wetly to my face.

She says, You lied to me.

I pour milk into the cup, take the teabag out and dispose of it in the bin.

For sure, I know this is true.

I look at her, and I say, I'm sorry.

I say, I was at rock bottom, and I just wanted to forget who I was for a little bit. Working with your dad, it just made me feel good again, you know?

I say, But when I found out how you felt about him, I was in too deep to be able to tell you the truth.

I say, I shouldn't have lied, I know that.

She's quiet, just sitting there, looking at me.

I say, The funny thing is, I came out here wanting to forget who I was. But instead, you actually helped me find myself – in a weird kind of way.

So thanks for that, I say.

She carries on looking at me. Her face is a complete blank.

I can't figure out what she's thinking, and the silence is torture.

She picks up her keys and her phone, gets up from the stool.

She looks me dead in the eye and she says, Fuck you, Sean. *Omae saitei da na, ningen no kuzu.*

And I watch as she leaves, the sharp click of her heels stabbing my poor, soft, squidgy brain.

Bye, Akemi, I say, after the door closes.

And once again, I am alone.

SIXTY

I knock on the door, one-two-three.

No answer.

I knock again, put my ear against the cold wood.

No sound.

A janitor clomps up the steps, and I point to the door and I say, Ta zai nali?

He looks at me and shrugs. Wo bu zhidao, he says, and carries on up the next flight of steps, dangling keys jangling.

I turn the knob, hear the latch click, feel the door giving in.

I walk down the hallway and into the living room, and it is even emptier than it was before. The brown leather sofa is gone, as is the giant print of the 101 and the light trails.

I go into the kitchen, it's empty.

I go into the bedroom, it's empty.

I go into the room where I watched Other Me reading his book at the desk in the light of a lamp. Those things too, they're gone.

But the flat, it doesn't feel empty, or cold. It just . . .

. . . is.

I raise my camera to my face, and I shoot.

* * *

As I walk down the street to the metro station, bag slung across my shoulder, I pass an old, beat-up electronics shop. In the dirt-smeared window there's a stack of vintage square TVs, eight wide and eight high.

The middle TVs, they're on. The screens, they're flashing blue and red, on account of the police car in the shot, parked outside the double-helix building.

I stop to watch, drop my bag. The reporter, she's talking emphatically, over-the-top gesturing with her hands. And although there's no sound, I can tell from the animated look on her face that she's reporting big news.

A little rectangle pops up in the top-right corner – footage from last night. It shows Charles, handcuffed and dishevelled – almost beyond recognition – being put into the back of a police car by a couple of cops.

Right before he gets into the car, he turns to stare right down the lens of the camera.

Eyes dead. Eyes cold.

I don't know how, but he's looking straight at me, looking straight into my eyes.

I pick up my bag, and I carry on walking.

Sixty-One

This is me, sitting on a row of metal chairs, waiting for my flight to London.

This is me, watching the people around me waiting, walking, boarding.

This is me, listening to the music of the airport announcements, the rise and the fall of the conversations going on around me.

In this moment in time, I am alone.

And I am, somehow, okay with that.

Don't get me wrong, I don't want to be alone. Who does?

But I think about Elliott Erwitt's picture, *Bratsk Wedding*, and the smiling dude.

The gaze directed out of frame, the chin cradled between thumb and forefinger.

I wonder whether it's my favourite picture not because it's stories for days, but because the dude, he knows something about himself that nobody else does.

For true, sitting here on my own, I think this is what I am waiting for.

That unmistakeable sense of clarity. That unmistakeable sense of me.

Until then, I am new, here.

And I want to document it.

To remember the significance of it.

To expose a bunch of silver halide crystals to refracted light, through a lens, just for a fraction of a second.

I watch a white businessman as he walks past. Tall, and confident. Strong, and handsome.

And I look at the Asians around me. Why are they so nerdy?

Anyway, where was I?

I lean over to the man sitting next to me, and I offer up my camera.

Do you mind? I say.

English, I say. Speak English?

As he raises my camera to his face, I say, Cheese.

The man though, he's got a puzzled look on his face. He's pushing and pushing the shutter button, but for some reason it won't budge.

I watch him frown, I watch him study the camera with his tongue poking out the side of his mouth.

And I think to myself that, of course, I am out of film.

ACKNOWLEDGEMENTS

Much love and gratitude:

Andrew Wille, ambassador of the non-grasp, whose teaching, guidance and support made this novel what it is, and me a better writer.

Zoe Ross, for her unwavering belief in this book and her artful feedback on the manuscript.

Kaiya Shang, for just getting it, and for her energy, passion and insight.

Chris White, for taking the reins so seamlessly and being such a pleasure to work with.

Olivia Davies, for holding the fort with such sensitivity and deftness.

Ella Fox-Martens, for her meticulous work on the manuscript.

Everyone at United Agents and Scribner UK.

Jack Smyth, for the stunning cover art.

Robert Dinsdale, for telling me to have a go at writing a novel, and for the continued advice and encouragement.

Kate Kemp, Ethan Darden, Sarah Springwater, Mouna Mounaya, Clare Milling, Sallie Clement, Theresa Ildefonso, Audrey Healy, Babatdor Dkhar and Michelle Garrett – for supporting my writing at an early stage and for reading an early draft of the manuscript.

My family.

And most of all, Ellie, Rowan and Bryher. For everything, thank you.